CURTAIN CALL

Inspector Casey Clunes' casebook includes many intriguing problems . . . In *Curtain Call*, an actress, Eloise Boucher, has disappeared and failed to turn up for the local theatre's evening performance. Casey's enquiries throw a spotlight on the owner of the theatre, hard-nosed Gwen Griffiths, her vain husband Caradoc and Eloise's friend and understudy, Pippa Jones. A body is found, but the discovery only makes the investigation more complicated . . . And in *Things Bad Begun*, even a weekend break in Cambridge proves that Casey is never off duty . . .

GERALDINE RYAN

CURTAIN CALL

Complete and Unabridged

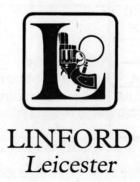

LINFORD
Leicester

First published in Great Britain

First Linford Edition
published 2012

British Library CIP Data

Ryan, Geraldine, *1951* –
    Curtain call.- -(Linford mystery library)
    1. Clunes, Casey (Fictitious character)- -
    Fiction. 2. Detective and mystery stories,
    English. 3. Large type books.
    I. Title II. Series III. Ryan, Geraldine,
    1951 – Things bad begun.
    823.9′2–dc23

    ISBN 978–1–4448–1150–6

Published by
F. A. Thorpe (Publishing)
Anstey, Leicestershire

Set by Words & Graphics Ltd.
Anstey, Leicestershire
Printed and bound in Great Britain by
T. J. International Ltd., Padstow, Cornwall

This book is printed on acid-free paper

Curtain Call

The call came in just as I was about to go for a break. Missing girl. Actress. Someone had to get down to the theatre pronto. And I was that lucky person. I'd been planning a canteen fry-up, but now it would have to wait. How come it was always me who got the hysterical females? For it had been a woman who'd rung in, according to my boss.

'I'd go myself,' McGovern said, when I reported to his office. 'Only I'm not feeling too pukka this morning.'

'Sorry to hear that, sir,' I lied.

Gov' McGovern was the biggest hypochondriac out. He didn't get headaches; he got brain tumours, and he'd had more meningitis scares than you could shake an aspirin bottle at. Funny thing, though, he never took a day off.

'Yeah. Upset stomach. Been plaguing me all morning.'

'Dodgy curry, sir? I heard they had the

food Inspectors in at The Maharani. Anonymous tip-off. Latest is, the closed sign's on the door.'

'Doesn't surprise me,' McGovern said. 'Personally, I've avoided that place ever since I found a hair in my biryani.'

He handed me the details of the mis-per. Eloise Boucher. Age twenty-two. Natural blonde. Blue eyes. Five seven and about nine stone in weight. Already I hated her.

'Call was received from Gwen Griffiths. Woman who owns the theatre.'

'Alongside her husband Caradoc.'

Gov looked impressed. 'Thought you'd be more into clubs and boozers,' he said.

'You can do all three if you know how,' I replied. If Gov thought I was a chav, I'd live with it.

'You'll know your way around the place, then?'

I nodded. The Gwen Griffiths Players performed a different play every fortnight and I saw most of them.

Casting my eye over the details, I said, 'Should have been in to do her performance last night but didn't show.

Landlady can't remember when she last saw her, according to Mrs Griffiths.'

'Correct.'

'Anything suspicious, sir, d'you think?'

'That's for you to find out.' Gov smirked.

Fine, I didn't need his help. At the door I turned round.

'IBS,' I said, smiling sweetly. 'Just a suggestion, Gov.'

He looked puzzled. 'Irritable bowel syndrome,' I explained.

Already he was reaching for his medical dictionary.

Gwen Griffiths was still an attractive woman. From the back row of the stalls. She still had that incredible voice, though. Rich and smoky, and a hint of a Welsh accent, with vowels hewn from rich black coal and not a dropped consonant anywhere.

'My dear young woman,' she snapped, by way of reply to my suggestion that Eloise Boucher might just have decided to take herself off on holiday without informing anyone first. 'Actors don't just not turn up for a performance.'

She lit a cigarette impatiently.

'When was the last time you saw her?' I asked.

'I thought I'd already said all that, when I phoned this morning,' she snapped.

'Just for the records,' I said in my best policewoman's voice.

She ran through the story again, seeming not so much worried by the girl's disappearance as annoyed and inconvenienced by it. She'd been there for the dress rehearsal the previous morning, but failed to turn up for her thirty-minute call in the evening, she said.

'Her understudy had to go on, you know,' she added, shuddering. 'God knows what sort of a review we've got. I daren't read the *Brockhaven Gazette*.'

'You weren't close to Miss Boucher, I take it?' I asked.

I knew actors were a self-centred bunch, but still it seemed a bit odd — putting reviews before your concerns over someone's safety.

'She's an employee, Miss . . . er . . . '

I'd flashed my badge on first meeting

her but she'd barely given it a cursory glance.

'Inspector Clunes,' I said. 'Casey Clunes.'

Her expression suggested she'd already dismissed the name.

'And how long had — has — she been a member of your company?' I corrected myself self-consciously.

A mobile phone went off.

'You'll probably find that's your missing actress,' I said.

'We can but hope.' She fished into the scuffed leather handbag hanging over the arm of her chair. From the curt way she addressed the speaker, it was obviously someone she had no interest in speaking to.

'Look, the police are here right now. Can't this wait?'

A female voice on the other end of the line responded. Gwen Griffiths rolled her eyes.

'No. No news. Believe me, you'll be the first to know.'

A barrage of words followed. Then Gwen Griffiths replied, 'I know I said we'd discuss it, but not now. I'll speak to you later.'

I thought I heard the other person say, 'When later?'

'Later, later,' Gwen Griffiths snapped. 'After I've finished speaking to the police.'

Gwen Griffiths tapped her foot impatiently as she listened to the caller speak again.

'Oh, all right then. You can help me walk that wretched dog of Caradoc's. Now, if you'll excuse me.'

Turning to me, she said, 'The understudy. It's an ill wind, Inspector, but the girl's all wrong for the part. And now she's talking about renegotiating her contract.'

'You're not keen, then,' I said.

'Girl's too inexperienced,' she replied. 'Although I hardly think you're here to discuss casting, Inspector.'

'You were about to tell me how long Eloise Boucher has worked in your company,' I replied, equally coolly.

'Look, Inspector, I'll make no bones about it.' Gwen Griffiths ground out her cigarette, adding it to the contents of an already overloaded ashtray. 'It was my husband who insisted she join the company and that was two months ago. She'd add a touch of glamour, he said. Just a pity she can't remember her lines and still doesn't seem to know the difference between stage left and stage right.'

Ah, so that was the way of things. Caradoc Griffiths. The old dog!

'Perhaps I should have a word with your husband,' I said. 'See if he can shed any light on Miss Boucher's disappearance.'

'I'm afraid that's not possible,' she said, affecting a charming smile that failed to convince. 'My husband's away at the moment.'

'Oh?'

She faltered but soon picked herself up. 'That's right. On business. Somewhere up north.'

She gestured wildly at an imaginary map, seemingly inviting me to identify Caradoc's location on it.

'We're looking for new sponsors,' she added. 'You wouldn't believe how much money this theatre swallows.'

'I'm sure,' I said.

Why did his wife sound so cagey at the mention of his name? I wondered. My mind was already jumping ahead. Sure, there was an age gap and a huge one at that. But what if Eloise and Caradoc had run off together? Stranger things happen in the world of showbiz, I reminded myself.

But if they had, why would his wife humiliate herself by calling in the police? It'd be all over the papers tomorrow. Unless. I racked my brains. What was the saying? All publicity was good publicity, that was it. A scandal like this might rock the marital boat, but it would also bring the punters in.

But if all this was a hoax, maybe it was time to remind Gwen Griffiths there was something called wasting police time.

'If you're trying to protect your husband for some reason, Mrs Griffiths,' I said, 'then I have to warn you you're making a big mistake.'

Gwen Griffiths looked startled. 'What on earth are you suggesting, Inspector?'

she said. Then her hand flew to her mouth. 'Gracious me! You think he did it, don't you?'

'You're a few jumps ahead of me,' I said. 'Did what, exactly?'

'Oh, come on, Inspector. Killed her, of course.'

She sounded remarkably cheerful, I thought.

'It's way too early for me to think a crime has been committed, Mrs Griffiths,' I said. 'Although the fact that you seem reluctant to inform me of your husband's location does concern me, frankly.'

In my job, you have to give people a chance to speak in their own time. It often means waiting but it usually pays off in the end. It did this time.

'I can see it's time to come clean, Inspector,' she said at last.

I pricked up my ears in anticipation.

'My husband has always been a foolish man where young girls are concerned,' she continued. 'In his younger days, he was quite a catch. Unfortunately, he never could bear to grow old.'

'I'm not sure I understand.'

'Two days ago,' she said, 'my husband checked into a private clinic to have some work done on his face.'

'A face lift?'

'Hard to believe how vain some people can be, isn't it, Inspector?'

She pushed a business card towards me, on which was written the address and phone number of a London clinic much favoured by celebrities.

'They did the operation yesterday at about midday,' she said. 'Of course, you don't have to take my word for it.'

We'd check it, of course.

'There's no way Caradoc would come prowling back here to do someone in, Inspector, if that's what you're thinking,' she said.

'Like I said, Mrs Griffiths,' I butted in. 'You're way ahead of me.'

'It takes time for surgery to heal,' she continued, 'and if my husband were going to murder a young girl, he'd want to make sure he was looking his best for her.'

I'd got to hand it to her. Here was a

woman who knew her husband inside out, warts and all. Not that he had any warts, as of yesterday.

'You'll find I'm telling the truth, Inspector,' she added. 'I booked it myself. And there's no way I'd write a cheque for that amount if I thought it was going on some floozy.'

I believed her. I decided it was time to make some more enquiries. Did Eloise Boucher have any enemies? I wondered. Looking like she did, it would hardly be surprising. Gwen Griffiths herself, even. I couldn't rid myself of the suspicion that the new face was intended for the girl and not the wife.

'By the way, Inspector,' she said, as I turned to leave. 'I know what you must think. But you're wrong. Eloise Boucher is a beautiful young woman who could have anyone she wanted. She wouldn't touch my husband with the proverbial barge pole.'

I didn't deign to reply. Instead, after promising to let her know immediately we heard anything, I headed out through the building to my car. It was time to interview Boucher's landlady, I decided, to find out what she knew. I was so deep in thought that I didn't register steps behind me until they were almost upon me and I heard a familiar voice.

'Hold up, Inspector. Can I have a word?'

Dom Talbot, journalist on the *Brockhaven Gazette*. I swore under my breath. No doubt he thought he was on to a scoop. Normally his byline came under reports of tedious council meetings and the like. He also did the reviews, which was how come I knew him. He'd been trying to get me to go out with him for months now and, whenever I turned up at a concert or a play, there he was too, propping up the bar in the interval just like me, small talk as sharp as his pencil.

He was all right, I suppose. Good-looking in a five o'clock-shadow, too-few-vitamins and too-many-late-nights kind of a way. But I wasn't looking for a boyfriend. I'd told him so — several times — and to his credit he never seemed to take offence.

'Inspector Clunes,' he said. 'So. What's the story?'

'There is no story,' I snapped. 'Not that that's ever stopped you from making one up.'

'Tut, tut, Inspector,' he went on. 'Ever heard the word libel?'

'Look, Dom,' I sighed. 'I'm hungry. My blood sugar's low and that always puts me in a bad mood.' I looked at my watch. Three o'clock. Way past my lunch-hour now. 'Ever heard the phrase 'obstructing the course of police duty'?'

He held out his arms, wrists to the fore. 'I promise I won't struggle if you want to slip the cuffs on,' he said, with a lascivious grin.

I glared back, tugging open my car door so it caught him a sharp blow in the ribs.

'Apologies,' I said. 'I was aiming lower.'

Then I started up the engine, fastened my seat belt and drove off.

Miss Grace had always taken in theatricals, as she called them.

'I suppose it has something to do with the fact that I had a yen to turn professional myself,' she said, as she poured out tea. 'Chocolate cake, dear?'

Already my mouth was watering.

'Of course, in my day, actresses were seen as barely respectable in the eyes of my mother. I had to make do with amateur dramatics.' She gave a wistful sigh before continuing. 'When she passed on, leaving this big old house to me, I decided I could either take in salesmen and sentence myself to a lifetime of dreary silence at the dinner table or I could finally introduce a bit of glamour to my hitherto staid existence.'

I asked her when she'd last seen Eloise Boucher.

'That's just it, Inspector,' she said. 'I can't for the life of me remember.'

16

I felt suddenly depressed. So far, the one lead I'd had had proved futile. Caradoc Griffiths, so I'd been informed on my way over to interview Miss Grace, hadn't been left unattended since he'd checked in at the clinic. So if anything had happened to Boucher, he hadn't had anything to do with it.

'Tell me about Eloise,' I said encouragingly.

'When she first arrived, oh, it was so lively here,' Miss Grace said, her eyes lighting up. 'In and out of each other's rooms, the girls were. Swapping clothes and make-up. But recently, it's grown very quiet.' She leaned forward and said, in a confidential manner, 'I rather think there was a fall out.'

'Who are these other girls?' I was suddenly curious.

'Oh, only one girl,' Miss Grace said. 'That's Miss Jones. Lovely girl! I believe she played Miss Boucher's part last evening in her — ' She hesitated, raking her internal thesaurus for a word that wouldn't offend — 'absence,' she concluded.

17

I made a mental note to get the lowdown on this Miss Jones as soon as. It must have been her on the phone to Gwen Griffiths, demanding to have her contract renegotiated. Bit keen, considering her best chum had disappeared off the face of the earth without leaving a message, I thought. Was this the enemy I'd been looking for?

I had every intention of having a good look round the ex-best friend's room while I was here, although I'd have to be casual about it. Miss Grace was a nice old bird and I didn't want to give her a scare by making her think she was renting a room to a murderer. Not that I was jumping to any conclusions just yet.

But it was getting hard not to think that something bad had happened to Eloise Boucher — and this so called chum of hers, Miss Jones, was as good a place to start as any. Checking my text messages while Miss Grace was out filling the kettle, I'd discovered that Eloise Boucher hadn't been to her parents' house in months. The last they'd heard from her was two days previously, when she'd told them how much she was looking forward to the first night.

If she was so excited about it then why on earth would she bale out at the last minute? Stage fright? I really didn't think so. There was no denying things were looking bleak.

'Perhaps I could have a look at Miss Boucher's room,' I suggested.

'Of course you must,' Miss Grace said. 'It's this way.'

I'd noticed, when she'd let me in, that Miss Grace had supported herself with an elegant, ivory, steel-tipped cane. I couldn't help thinking, as I followed her up the stairs, that oddly enough this accessory, along with her slight limp, added to her gracefulness, rather than detracted from it. Gwen Griffiths could learn a thing or two from this classy broad, I mused.

'Here we are, Inspector. Miss Boucher's room.'

If Eloise Boucher had left in a hurry, there was no sign of it. Her few clothes, all size ten with good labels, hung neatly in her wardrobe, her bed had been made and there wasn't so much as a used cotton-wool pad on her dressing table.

Something was niggling me. What was it Miss Grace had said earlier? In and out of each other's rooms? I found myself growing more impatient by the second to speak to Miss Jones — Pippa Jones, now that I remembered.

I'd seen her photo in the foyer with all the rest. How would I describe her? A broad face, cat's eyes, big, lustrous hair. Attractive? Not in Eloise Boucher's class but there wouldn't be that many would kick her out of bed.

Just then, my phone rang. 'You'd better get down here,' McGovern said. 'They've found a body. Looks like it's your actress.'

* * *

The girl lay crookedly at the foot of the cliffs. The place was crawling with uniform running around with ticker tape and Forensics were out in force.

I spotted Gov immediately. He wasn't looking that good, actually. But I wasn't here to ask after his health. I raised my eyes to the cliff tops. Not many people used the path that led down to this secluded cove, at any time of the year. Maybe you'd get the odd jogger or a local out walking the dog. Tourists wouldn't fancy it though because there was no ice-cream van and no bus to take them back to their hotels.

'So. Did she fall or was she pushed?'

'Forensics won't say,' he said darkly.

Gov always took Forensic's natural caution as a personal slight. He seemed to think they wanted the glory for themselves and blamed Sam Ryan on the telly for turning them into prima donnas.

'Take a look.'

I didn't know what I'd expected when he lifted the cover and revealed her face. But it wasn't this.

'This isn't Eloise Boucher, sir,' I said. 'This is her understudy. Pippa Jones.'

Gov glared at me for a full ten silent seconds. Finally he spoke.

'There's no ID on her,' he snapped. 'Missing female about twenty-five years old, we were told. How many can there be in a place this big?'

'It's an easy mistake to make, sir,' I

said, dwelling just a little longer than necessary on the word 'mistake'.

'You're going to have to go back to the theatre and interview the entire company,' he went on. 'This business is getting more complicated by the minute.'

Talk about understatement. For the second time that day, I drove to the theatre. I parked outside the stage door. Wouldn't you just know that Dom Talbot would be hanging around outside like some Stage Door Johnny?

'Before you ask, I've no comment,' I said, sweeping past him.

'Aw, come on, Casey,' he groaned after me. 'Give us a break.'

He sounded fed up. He looked fed up. His brown leather jacket was turned up at the collar to ward off the damp wind. A lock of hair flopped over his forehead, giving him the look of a little boy lost. I felt sorry for him.

I sighed. 'The body of a young woman has been found,' I said. 'She'd fallen from the cliffs.'

My news clearly revived him. His whole face lit up. You'd think I'd told him he'd landed an exclusive with Michael Jackson.

'No kiddin'!' he yelped. 'Eloise Boucher? Suicide? Or murder? Any signs of sexual activity?'

'And there was I confusing you with a human being for a minute there,' I said.

When I added that Eloise Boucher was still missing and the body was that of Pippa Jones, Dom let out a long, low whistle.

'Don't go jumping to conclusions,' I cautioned him. 'We all know what a fertile imagination you journalists have. Now, if you'll excuse me, I have to see a woman about a body.'

I pushed past him, leaving him standing open-mouthed behind me.

Curtain call

Gwen Griffiths was remarkably subdued. Clearly, she'd already been informed of the news. I found her where I'd left her — sitting at her desk in her office, calmly smoking a cigarette and drinking whisky from a large tumbler. When I walked in she looked up briefly, then, addressing her glass, she said, voice slightly slurred, 'Never before, in the history of this theatre company, have we ever had to cancel a performance. First the leading lady goes missing. Next her understudy turns up dead.'

I couldn't believe I'd heard right. Had she given one thought to the victim in this, or to the victim's family? I was suddenly overcome with fury at her callousness but was prevented from giving her a piece of my mind by a knock at the door, which opened to reveal the detective constable who'd been sent to help me interview the cast.

'Urgent message from the nick, Inspector. I think you'll want to get down there. I've been ordered to stay and begin the interviews. The cast are assembled in the stalls.'

What, I wondered, was Gov playing at? All I'd done so far was drive backwards and forwards, achieving nothing at all. How was I expected to find a murderer doing that?

'So what's the big surprise?'

I was on my mobile as soon as I was outside. I'd left a different way to avoid bumping into Talbot again.

'It's Eloise Boucher.' Gov sounded even tetchier than usual. 'She's alive. And she has something to tell us.'

'You mean she's down the nick?'

I couldn't think straight. Why had she gone there? Surely, if she had some apologising to do for missing her first night — which Gwen Griffiths for one would say she had — she would have gone straight to the theatre?

Unless . . . What if she'd gone to the nick because she had something to confess?

* * *

Even without a scrap of make up, Eloise Boucher was a stunner. McGovern, by contrast, looked dreadful. He'd discarded his jacket and his sweat-stained, crumpled shirt strained across his flabby stomach. His brow glistened with sweat and every now and then he gave a wince of pain.

They both stood up as I came into the interview room.

'What's going on, Gov?' I said impatiently.

He gestured towards a chair and sat down again himself. Eloise Boucher, however, remained standing. Obviously she didn't trust me. Briefly, I introduced myself.

'Just tell the Inspector what you told me,' Gov said. 'But tell it from the beginning. Not the end.'

'First of all,' she said, taking her seat again, 'I should explain my absence.'

'Well, it might be a start,' I said. 'Seeing as most of our officers have been out looking for you all day. Not to mention your landlady, who's worried sick about where you may be.'

Gov gave me a look. Obvious he was besotted with her already. But I was a woman. I wasn't so easy to charm. Her story had better be good, that was all I could say.

'But I told Miss Grace I was going to go away for a while,' she protested.

'She's an old lady,' I said, brushing her excuse aside. 'She's probably losing her hearing.'

'Miss Grace's hearing is perfect,' Eloise Boucher protested. 'In fact, I've rarely met anyone with such a good ear.'

'Time's ticking by, Miss Boucher,' I snapped. 'And I've yet to hear your story.'

'Of course,' she said. She swallowed hard and began. 'I thought that if I disappeared for a couple of days, Gwen Griffiths would have no option but to give Pippa my part.'

I did a mental double-take. So this disappearing act was all about doing her understudy a favour? Yeah, and I still believed in the tooth fairy.

She acknowledged it must sound weird. But Pippa was her best friend, she insisted, and she was fed up with the way Gwen Griffiths treated her, never giving her any opportunity to show her ability.

Mentally, I stroked the nugget of information I'd been given this afternoon by Eloise Boucher's landlady. There'd been a falling out between the girls, she'd hinted. Best friend, was she saying? Ha! Someone was telling porkies or I was a vegetarian.

'Gwen Griffiths knew Caradoc was besotted with Pippa, you see,' Eloise went on. 'She was hardly likely to give her any more opportunity to work with her husband than she already had.'

'Caradoc King fancied Pippa Jones?'

Pippa Jones was the love object, not Eloise Boucher? This was taking me a while to get my head round.

'Was it mutual, this attraction?' I added.

'What do you think, Inspector?' she replied, scornfully.

'When did you speak to Pippa last?' I wanted to know.

'Yesterday,' she said. 'Just before she was killed, I guess . . . '

Then she told me her story. The previous day, after the dress rehearsal, she said, she'd travelled to a B and B in Lowestoft — which, after a nod from Gov, I gathered had been checked out as kosher. All this she'd planned together with Pippa to make sure her friend the understudy got her chance to play the leading role.

'Who's idea was this initially?' I wanted to know. So far we only had Boucher's word for any of this. If she thought I was trying to trip her up, she didn't show it.

Freely, she admitted the plan had been hers. She was fed up with acting, she said.

'I was rubbish,' she said. Her eyes welled up with tears. 'Poor Pippa. She could have been great. I told her to make sure Gwen Griffiths realised it, by hounding her to give her the part for the rest of the run.'

Could I believe her? If you believed Gwen Griffiths, Eloise Boucher was no actress. But those tears were real. You couldn't fake 'em. Annoyingly, I believed her. Because something else was niggling me. Something that tied all this to Gwen Griffiths. Something to do with Pippa Jones. Mentally I groped my way towards it. That was it! Pippa Jones and a phone call.

'I was there,' I said, suddenly remembering. 'When she rang up Gwen Griffiths. She asked to meet her. To talk about it. But Griffiths said she was too busy.'

I racked my brains. Busy with what? What did she have to do that wouldn't wait? Something about a dog. That's right. She had to take Caradoc's dog for a walk.

And Pippa Jones knew this. Did she decide to go to meet Griffiths on her walk? To persuade her that she should give her another chance? But that was a ridiculous idea! Brockhaven wasn't a large town. Even so you'd have to know where to go to meet someone and Griffiths hadn't specified her route. Unless . . .

'Who usually took Caradoc's dog for walkies?' I asked.

'Anyone who could be persuaded,' Eloise said. 'Or bribed. I've done it myself a few times.'

'And was it always the same route?'

'Across the common, up the old cliff road and along the tops.'

So it would have been no trouble for Pippa Jones to search out Griffiths and take up the discussion where she'd left off? And, up there, on the cliffs, with not a soul in sight, how simple it would have been for Griffiths to push the girl over the edge, and to shut her up forever. That way, she'd have her Peter Pan husband all to herself again. And no one would be any the wiser.

'Thank you, Miss Boucher,' I said.

'You've been most helpful.'

I was sorry I wasn't going to be the one to bring Griffiths in. But I'd see her in the interview room soon enough, I reasoned. Meanwhile I drank a coffee with Eloise Boucher, allowing her to chat on aimlessly, hoping it might make her feel better, even in a small way. She spoke of the laughs they'd had. Not just Pippa and herself but Miss Grace too.

'I still can't get my head round it,' she said. 'Poor Pippa.'

Me neither. It would have been — what time, when Pippa Jones phoned Griffiths? I racked my brains. I remembered bumping into Dom Talbot when I left the theatre and checking my watch.

Three o'clock. That was it! Way past my lunch time, I'd said. From there I'd gone to interview Miss Grace. I was at her house a few minutes later. I got the call from the scene before three-thirty. To my knowledge, Pippa Jones had been lying there at least forty minutes.

I stared into the bottom of my mug. Something wasn't right. I hated to have to admit it to myself but there was no way

31

Gwen Griffiths could have pushed that girl over the cliff. A chill ran through me. It might have sounded crazy but it was beginning to look like Gwen Griffiths had received a call from a girl who was already dead.

'I should get back.'

Eloise Boucher's voice roused me from my reverie.

'I told Miss Grace I'd be back for dinner tonight,' she said.

This was the second time she'd told me she'd mentioned either her planned absence or her expected return to her landlady. Yet Miss Grace had said nothing about either of these things.

The phone rang. Forensics thought that Pippa Jones had been dead since about eight a.m. this morning.

'An accident then?' Gov said, when I called him to relay the news. 'Lets Gwen Griffiths off the hook at least.'

I didn't hear what else he said. Something about her looking the type to sue for wrongful arrest. Something about his gut ache getting worse. Blah blah blah. Eloise Boucher stood up and mouthed that she was leaving.

Slamming down the phone, I leaped up, spilling my half full cup of undrinkable canteen coffee, and ran after her.

'Miss Boucher,' I said, when I finally caught up with her. 'Congratulations. I think you've solved my case.'

★ ★ ★

In the end Lavinia Grace came quietly. Because it had been Miss Grace who'd rung up Gwen Griffiths, albeit in the guise of Pippa Jones. She knew exactly what to say, of course, because she'd been present throughout Eloise and Pippa's many conversations in which they'd planned exactly how to persuade their reluctant employer to allow Pippa to keep the leading role in the new production.

Her motive?

'I loved Caradoc, Inspector,' she told me later, when she'd been brought in for questioning. 'I'd always loved him since we started acting in amateur dramatics together, before he moved on and met that woman.'

I assumed 'that woman' was his wife. Ten years Miss Grace's junior, apparently, Griffiths had swept him off his feet instantly. The couple later opened their theatre, turned pro and the rest was history.

'Why did you kill Pippa Jones, Miss Grace?' I asked.

'It must be hard for you to imagine, Inspector,' she said, a sad smile playing on her face. 'But all the time Pippa Jones was ridiculing Caradoc's oafish behaviour towards her, even though I joined in the laughter and agreed with the girls that older men were fools where young women were concerned, my heart bled with tenderness and pity for him.'

Not seeing someone for the silly, vain old fool that the rest of the world saw him as — yes, that sounded like love to me.

'I don't think that I was aware of my intentions, Inspector,' she continued,' but when I asked Pippa to forgo her usual early morning jog this morning and take me for a ride in her car along the cliffs, subconsciously I think I knew what I was going to do.'

Jones, in an ebullient mood after her performance of the night before had willingly agreed to change her routine for once, according to Miss Grace. Once parked, the two of them made their way along the cliffs, admiring the view.

'She was looking out to sea,' Miss Grace explained. 'I pushed her with the tip of my cane. She'd poked fun at Caradoc once too often and whereas before I'd managed to control my loathing of her, this time I couldn't.'

Then, a miraculous thing occurred. Right in front of my eyes she seemed to shed years and in a girlish voice — Pippa Jones's voice, I assumed — she said, 'As if I'd bother with that silly old man.' Speaking in her own voice now, she added, 'It was then I pushed her off the edge of the cliff. A bigger girl would have resisted, but she was just a feather of a thing.'

She'd driven back home in Pippa Jones's car, stopping at the car wash. Back home she'd cleaned her cane and boots and tried to think of a way to get out of the mess she knew she was in.

She'd no idea what she was doing, but by phoning Gwen Griffiths and pretending to be Pippa, she'd hoped at least to throw the police off her scent until she came up with a plan. It had very nearly worked, to give the old girl her due.

Now, I was on my way home. It had been a long day.

A figure loomed up out of the shadows as I trailed, exhausted, towards my car. Talbot again! Did he ever sleep? It must have been exhaustion that made me give him the story.

'Wow!' he exclaimed, when I'd finished. Then, always the chancer, he added, 'You must feel like celebrating!'

'With you, you mean? Apart from the fact that I'm practically sleep-walking, I can't think of one single bar that stays open so late in Brockhaven,' I said.

'There's always my place,' he replied.

I'd walked into that one, I suppose. Thankfully, I was saved from refusing by the wailing siren and flashing lights of an ambulance shrieking down the road in our direction. It pulled up just behind us and from each door a paramedic leapt, hurtling towards the front entrance of the Police Station.

'Blimey! What's the rush?' Dom said.

My phone rang. It was the duty officer. When he told me the news, I yelped.

It was Gov. He hadn't been joking this time about being ill. Only it wasn't IBS. He'd only gone and got appendicitis, hadn't he? Collapsed with pain in the men's toilets. Poor old Gov!

'Two big stories in one night,' Dom said, impressed. 'Now, that does deserve a celebration. What about dinner tomorrow? I bet you're a curry fan. Everyone likes a curry.'

'OK,' I said. 'The Maharani at eight. I'll see you outside.'

'Brilliant,' he said. He looked well chuffed. Of course, if he hadn't been so busy trailing after me all day, and kept his ear a bit nearer the ground, he'd have known The Maharani was no more, thanks to the health Inspectors slapping a big fat *Closed until further notice* sign on it. He'd find out tomorrow night at eight, though, which meant I still had a good few hours to decide whether to let him stew on his own outside, or phone him and tell him it was a wind up.

There was a third option, of course. I could book somewhere else on the off chance he'd forgive me for my little prank. Well, we all deserved a break once in a while. Even Dom Talbot.

All In A Summer Season

'Mark my words, you'll soon be on the lookout for a man to share all that space with,' my boss, 'Gov' McGovern said, when I told him I'd exchanged my poky flat for a five-roomed apartment right in the heart of Brockhaven, the seaside resort where I lived and worked as a Detective Inspector in the Brockhaven Police Force.

'I don't think Mrs McGovern would be very happy about that arrangement, do you, sir?' I replied, with a gracious smile.

It was a principle of mine to take at least one swipe at McGovern every day. There was no satisfaction greater than watching his smug smile freeze on his whiskery face, while he tried to work out how to climb out of the hole he'd quite voluntarily dug himself into.

I'd been in my flat for one whole month now and, very gradually, it was coming together. I'd gone way over budget on curtains, but had easily convinced myself that such a magnificent bay window — looking out over the entire length of the High Street as it did — was a feature that couldn't be exaggerated.

Gradually, I picked up a chair here, a cushion there, a mirror somewhere else. The eclectic look, Dom Talbot, my boyfriend, called it, when I eventually allowed him inside to take a look.

Dom was a journalist on the *Brockhaven Gazette*. Words were his thing and there probably hadn't been that many opportunities for him to use ones like 'eclectic' in the pieces that he wrote.

Anyway, now my flat was looking dandy, any reservations I'd initially had about saddling myself with such a huge mortgage were beginning to dissolve. If there was one small cloud on the horizon, it was this. Summer had arrived in Brockhaven and with it the tourists.

That meant traffic, both the human and the motorised variety. Up and down the High Street all day it roared and chattered, disturbing the routine of the locals, who'd only just got used to having the place to themselves again after the last lot had gone home.

I was a city girl. Considering how foreign the small-town atmosphere had been to me when I'd first arrived in Brockhaven, it was weird that one month into the season I was beginning to miss the slow pace of life I'd got accustomed to.

Only that afternoon, I'd been forced to queue for fifteen minutes in the chemist's, which had made me late for an appointment, and getting from one end of the High Street to the other was a major manoeuvre. On top of everything else, I never seemed to see the same faces twice.

'It's all wrong,' I said to Dom, as I pushed the vinegar bottle across the table towards him, one early summer evening as we sat at my kitchen table eating fish and chips. 'It's as if your granny's suddenly developed a drug habit or decided to go in for plastic surgery without consulting the family first.'

'Look, I can see you're tired. If you want, I'll go once we've finished these,' he said. 'Was it kids larking about again?'

I nodded. 'First time in weeks I managed to get to bed before eleven and I was kept awake till nearly two.'

'Couldn't you have stuck your head out of the living room window and told them to keep the noise down?' Dom wanted to know.

'I did,' I told him. 'Well, I got up, peeped from behind the curtain to see what I could see. Which wasn't much. Some mild horseplay. Couple of kids arguing. A bit of snogging. Cast your mind back to your own misspent youth and I'm sure you'll catch my drift. Then I went back to bed.'

'You should have threatened to arrest them,' Dom said with a grin.

Like most men, Dom thought that every problem had a solution. He just didn't get it that sometimes all we women wanted was a good old moan. In fact, we preferred it. At the end of the day, a problem solved was a problem you'd never again be given a second opportunity to moan about.

I chased my last chip around my plate with the wooden fork I'd insisted on to save the washing-up.

'Don't listen to me,' I said with a sigh. 'I'm just knackered, that's all. Sorry if I sound like Disgusted of Brockhaven.'

I refrained from filling Dom in on the report I'd been working on earlier about the changing demographics of visitors to Brockhaven. I'd already decided that it was pure speculation, anyway, but that morning when I'd discussed it with McGovern, he'd had a very different point of view.

'The writing's on the wall,' McGovern had warned me as I'd presented him with the statistics.

'Once prices start going up or the local youth start finding it difficult to get a seat at their local, it'll be Mods and Rockers all over again. Yob culture, antisocial behaviour, orgies, binge drinking, drugs, you name it, they'll be doing it.'

The usual holidaymakers had been young families or, at the other end of the scale, retired people. This new breed of tourist were teenagers who'd been coming here for a week or two every summer with their well-heeled, middle-class parents since they'd been in nappies. They knew their way around; they had access to their parents' holiday cottages.

In small numbers that was fine. We had never expected trouble and we'd never had any. But these kids had pals whom they were inviting back in droves to let their hair down after they'd done their A-levels — this was before the little darlings embarked on the gruelling slog of their gap year, you understand. Mix them up with those kids who'd lived in Brockhaven all their lives and to whom the phrase 'gap year' meant unemployment, and you had a worrying recipe for potential mayhem.

Sometimes, I mused, laying down my fork at last, I wished Dom did any other job but the one he did. I'd have liked to chew this report over with him. The problem was, he was a journalist to his bones. What would he do with the news that Brockhaven was about to be invaded by a horde of toff teenagers? Unwittingly, I'd even written part of his snappy copy for him. It'd be splashed all over the front page in no time and we'd be inundated with complaints from angry residents demanding drastic measures.

Well, I decided, he wasn't going to hear it from me. Anyway, if this summer was as bad as the last, the visiting youth had the advantage over the locals in that they could afford to chase the sun. Let's hope they made that choice, I mused inwardly.

True to his word, Dom left soon after we'd finished eating. I didn't know whether to be flattered by his concern or insulted when he said it was obvious I needed my beauty sleep. He must have been right, though, because as soon as my head hit the pillow I fell fast asleep. I may have half-woken when the pubs spilled out their squealing, shrieking clientele. But, exhausted as I was, I wasn't planning on doing anything about the noise tonight. I was strictly off duty. Telling myself not to be such a spoilsport, I turned over and went back to sleep.

But when I got into work next day, McGovern was pacing the floor, taking sips of scalding hot coffee as he went. He looked haggard. Well, more haggard than usual, I mean.

'Have a bad night, sir?' I enquired coolly.

McGovern was a hypochondriac *par excellence*. It was always best to get details of his latest life-threatening disease out in the open immediately, then you could get on with the day ahead. Occasionally, though, he actually was ill. Last year he'd had a grumbling appendix, which had turned into peritonitis. According to the medical team who'd nursed him through it, it had been a close call. Since then I'd made sure to give at least a minute of my time every day to his accounts of his latest gruesome symptoms.

'You could say that,' McGovern said. 'Flamin' kids. Building bonfires on the beach. Playing their music all night. God knows what else was going on. A few of the locals came along and put their twopenn'orth in.'

It had started, then.

'Did you make any arrests?'

McGovern took a gulp of his coffee and made a face. 'Cautioned a few of the locals, warned the posh kids about using the beach as a venue for an all-night party. Think they know the consequences

48

if anything like it happens again.'

'Let's hope so,' I thought, as McGovern made his way back to his office, muttering something about kids who should go to Faliraki if all they wanted to do was get drunk and cause a riot.

For the rest of my shift, I couldn't help worrying about how things might escalate, particularly as today was Saturday and that meant there'd be more visitors coming down to the coast, particularly as the weather forecast was a good one.

Later, being lucky enough to have an unaccustomed Saturday evening off, I met Dom for a drink in the garden of The Lord Nelson.

'This is a nightmare,' Dom complained, as he raked the tables with his eyes for a place to sit.

'You go and get them in,' I said. 'I'll try to find somewhere to sit.'

By the time Dom reappeared with our beer, which was a good fifteen minutes later, I'd managed — by dint of pretending to be unaware that the young couple at our table would clearly have preferred it if we'd taken our pints elsewhere — to find us somewhere to sit.

'What's happened to this place?' he said, squeezing into the space I'd saved him. 'You and me must be the oldest here!'

'Don't rub it in,' I growled, with a sidelong glance at the female half of the couple we'd been forced to share a table with.

She looked kind of familiar, but then I guess she was a type. Golden skin she certainly hadn't acquired in Brockhaven and plenty of it on show. Lots of shiny-shiny hair that she kept tossing back from her face whenever she spoke. Legs up to her armpits, and when she wasn't fiddling with a cigarette packet she was fiddling with her mobile phone. 'Nervous,' I thought. I had the impression she'd have preferred her hands to be firmly locked inside those of her male companion, but he clearly wasn't having any.

For all his good looks, his tan and his expensive clothes, there was something about the boyfriend I found distinctly unattractive. Call it inverted snobbery on my part. I was a working-class girl and this guy, with his sulky mouth and the arrogant way he held his cigarette, was putting me right off my pint.

He'd clearly been there, done that and got the designer T-shirt, though he couldn't have been more than nineteen years old. I didn't like the way he barely seemed to listen to anything the girl said, either. His restless eyes lighted on one spot for a moment, then flickered and moved on. Did he ever look her straight in the eye? I wondered.

'We don't need to stay here, you know,' Dom said, observing my disdain.

He'd drained most of his pint already, and I wouldn't have blamed him for not relishing a return visit to the bar. Besides, there was something kind of crumpled about him this evening, which I was finding oddly attractive. I had beer in my fridge. A Saturday evening together was a rare thing. Especially when neither of us had to be up early the next day.

I should have thought more carefully when, in answer to Dom's question, your place or mine, I opted for the former. But

I was thinking of my huge bath with the copper taps, which was quite big enough for two if you knew what you were doing. I was remembering my double bed with the cool, newly-laundered sheets I suspected wouldn't be on offer at Dom's place. I asked myself, too, how safe would it be to walk about Dom's living room barefoot, considering his pistachio habit?

In retrospect, opting for my place wasn't, perhaps, the best choice. Dom's tiny but picturesque Edwardian cottage was a few miles out of Brockhaven, on a sleepy road in the middle of nowhere. We'd have managed a night's uninterrupted sleep if we'd driven over there and if we hadn't then we'd have only had ourselves to blame.

But situated slap bang in the High Street, as I was, meant there was no escaping the racket, as a couple of hours later Brockhaven's visiting teenagers — mingling with the local youth — spilled out of the pubs, all converging on the High Street at the same time.

'Come back to bed, Casey,' Dom implored from the bedroom. 'It's just a few kids having a laugh.'

Attracted by the noise, I'd wandered out of the bedroom in my bathrobe and had been standing in the dark of my living room, gazing down over the full length of the High Street for some minutes now.

I was restless. If something was about to kick off, I wanted to be in a position where I could see exactly what happened. Tempting as it was, joining Dom back in bed was not an option just now. He might have been a reporter to his bones. Well, I was a copper — with a copper's instincts. And my instinct told me things were getting ugly.

Turning my head for a split second to reply to Dom's plaintive request, I missed who it was threw the first insult. But the boy who threw the first punch was someone I knew very well — in a professional capacity, I hasten to add.

Liam Barford. Offences for 'twoccing' — that's joyriding — in his early teens, cautioned many times for under-age drinking and with a violent streak that was manifesting itself this very moment.

Mesmerised, I watched him swing a punch in the direction of a young man, who was now holding his bloody nose and struggling to get up from his knees.

I was on my mobile immediately, debating whether I should get down there myself and try to stop it before it all got out of hand or wait for back-up. The call made, I rushed back into the bedroom where, struggling into my discarded clothes, I described to Dom what I'd seen. Dom was on his feet straight away, making a lunge for his own clothes. It was while he was cursing because he didn't have his camera with him, that we heard the first bottle break.

Of course, with all the mayhem that ensued I had no option but to go in to work.

'Bang goes my morning off,' I informed Dom, as I slipped my shoes on.

'No worries.' Dom was at the window himself now. 'Gives me time to work on my exclusive — *Toff teenagers tyrannise townsfolk.*'

'I can almost hear the capital letters,' I groaned as I let myself out.

At the police station, it was hard to differentiate between the victims and the culprits. Barford, I'd witnessed with my own eyes, so, with the order to the desk sergeant to process them all, I invited Barford for a little chat.

'I demand a solicitor,' he yelled, as he was frogmarched to one of the interview rooms by PC Jimmy Patterson, a wide-eyed young man who'd hitherto had nothing more exciting to do than to return lost property to grateful old ladies.

'You've been watching too many episodes of *The Bill*, Liam,' I told him. 'It'll take a good four hours for us to get a solicitor out to Brockhaven. Now if you don't mind sleeping on a cell floor while we put a call out, then that's fine by me. Or we could just charge you and let you go home.'

He blinked a few times while he thought about it.

'Charge me with what, though?' he said triumphantly. 'I never did nothing. I was just there, innit?'

I flourished my mobile phone at him.

'Take a look at this photo, Liam,' I said.

'Some quick-witted passer-by thought that it might make a nice snapshot for his album.'

In this business, you soon learned to be devious. If I'd told Barford it was me who took the picture, he'd work out soon enough for himself exactly where I'd taken it from. What were the chances of him deciding to take his revenge on my lovely bay window once he did? And if I'd told Dom, we'd have ended up having a scrap ourselves, because he'd have wanted access to it for his scoop, which clearly would have been out of the question at such an early stage.

Confronted with the evidence, Barford didn't exactly say that it was a fair cop, but his body language suggested it. In no time he'd been charged and was freed on bail.

'He shouldn't have opened his posh mouth,' was all he said, in mitigation, as he left the room.

It was late when we'd finished interviewing everyone. Barford's victim insisted he wasn't badly hurt and his reluctance to follow it up suggested to me that he hadn't been quite as innocent as he'd appeared.

By three o'clock, we'd done and I was back in bed. Dom had left, leaving only a scrawled note behind.

Got some great pics of the debris. Off home to write copy. Cheers. Dom.

My phone woke me some six hours later.

'You're needed down on the beach, by Gunners' Green. Pronto,' McGovern snapped. 'There's been a body washed up on the sands. About an hour ago. Female.'

Already my heart was pumping and the adrenaline was starting to flow.

'Local?'

'No ID. Your guess is as good as mine.'

Down at the scene, there were already a few sightseers. From the corner of my eye, I spotted Liam Barford and a few of his equally scabby mates enjoying the spectacle of police and forensics swarming over the area.

A small white tent had been erected over the body, to shield it from prying eyes. Looking down at it I knew, even in its bloated, barely human shape, that this was the body of the girl I'd been sitting next to in The Lord Nelson the previous night. Then, she'd been dressed in her finery, her golden hair a testament to some West End stylist and her tan courtesy of years of foreign holidays.

Now, her hair was matted with sea-weed, her limbs were the colour of porridge and, bar a minuscule pair of briefs, she was naked. What had happened to the rest of her clothes? I wondered. It was doubt-ful that we'd find them if the sea had sucked them up and spat them out some other place.

'It's an accident, right?' I asked a grumpy-looking Dr Sparks, who clearly hadn't been too impressed by his early-morning wake-up call.

'Oh, very likely,' he said grudgingly. 'There's some grazing here — and here — some bruising round the neck. Probably occurred as she was buffeted by the tide.'

'So no inquest then?'

'No suspicious circumstances as far as I can tell,' Dr Sparks said. 'I just wish people would learn to treat the elements with a bit more respect.'

My phone suddenly sprang to life. It was PC Wilkinson, the desk sergeant.

'Got a young man down here. He's in a bit of a state. Says it's his girlfriend. She's gone missing.'

My stomach gave a lurch. 'I'm on my way,' I said.

The last time I'd seen Linus Goff-Whitham had been in very different circumstances. Then, he'd appeared in control and looked so cool you'd need an overcoat on before you could get near him.

Now, he sat hunched over a cup of station tea and the tanned complexion I remembered from the pub had been replaced by a shocked pallor. There was no recognition of me on his part, but then I was used to that. On duty, I tried to look anonymous.

I asked him when he had first discovered that his girlfriend was missing.

'Just this morning,' he said. 'I woke up and she wasn't in the house.'

'Would this be your house, sir?'

He shook his head and said it belonged to his parents. Bury Cross, he said it was called. I'd often passed it as I'd walked

59

along the front. A huge white pile, not far from Gunners' Green. You couldn't miss it. It was the size of a small hotel.

'But we're staying there — Annelise and me,' he added.

Sitting there, the cup resting in his hands, he looked, for a brief moment, achingly vulnerable beneath the hard veneer.

'Your parents — and hers — do they know you're staying at the house together?'

'Sure,' he said, with a casual shrug. 'They're cool about it.'

He set the cup down on the plastic-topped table beside him. I waited while he shifted position a couple of times before finding one to suit him. His restlessness suggested he had something to say that wasn't going to be easy.

'We had a row,' he said eventually, avoiding my eyes. 'That's why I wasn't worried till now. I thought she was probably sleeping in one of the other bedrooms. But when I woke up this morning and looked around she was nowhere.'

Sooner or later I was going to have to tell him what we'd found. But first I needed to know more. What had she been doing in the water half-naked, for one thing? And where had he been when the accident occurred?

'You haven't told me yet when you last saw Annelise,' I said.

'We'd been drinking. At The Lord Nelson.'

'Well, that much is definitely true,' I thought.

'Maybe that's why we started rowing. I don't really know, but alcohol can sometimes do that to Annelise. On the way home from the pub, she started to have a go at me.'

'How do you mean?'

'You know,' he said. 'Nagging. So, about — what — tennish, I said, let's go back home. I didn't want a row in a public place and besides I didn't like the atmosphere in the pub. Place was full of chavs, leering at Annelise. She couldn't see it, of course, but then she has no idea of the effect she has on men.'

He seemed to lose himself for a moment.

61

'So you went back home together, then?'

'Yes.'

'And was Annelise still — nagging — you?'

He tipped his chair backwards and stretched his long chino-clad legs, crossing his tanned arms over his chest. It was a defensive action. Clearly, he'd sensed my disapproval of his choice of vocabulary. He wasn't entirely without sensitivity then.

'Well, it wasn't really nagging. Like I said, Annelise was drunk. You know what lightweights girls are.'

I restrained myself from laying odds that I could drink him under the table.

'She fell asleep on the settee. I watched a DVD. When it had finished, she woke up and suggested we went for a swim.'

'She'd forgotten that she wasn't speaking to you, then?'

He raised his eyes heavenwards. 'Girls,' he said.

'What are we like?' I replied, like he was my best pal.

'So when did you eventually go for

your dip?' I asked him.

'I don't know. It would have been about two-ish, I guess. Very late, anyway. There was no one else about. So we just took off our clothes and waded in.'

I leaned forward and said, as gently as I could, 'Tell me, Linus. Do you have a photo of your girlfriend on you at all?'

Since Annelise's family lived in Hampstead, it was up to the Met to break the news to her parents, which was something I felt hugely grateful for. Seeing Annelise's bloated body, barely recognisable from the beautiful young woman I'd seen with my own eyes not twenty-four hours previously, had shocked me, I had to admit. Linus Goff-Whitham had appeared equally shaken up on hearing the news. I'd left him with a female PC, who had been given orders to stay with him until his friends came over. His parents were flying back from holiday to be near him, too.

The morning turned into the afternoon and I shuffled paper, while at the same time musing upon the supreme arrogance of the young. I guess I'd been just like

Goff-Whitham and his girlfriend, too, in my younger days, thinking I was invincible. But, tragically, the facts were that if you drank too much and then swam out of your depth, chances of a happy ending weren't going to be high. Unfortunately, the girl wasn't going to be around to learn the lesson.

Some time after lunch, I got a summons from my boss. Liam Barford had been brought in again and was cutting up rough. The young man he'd assaulted outside my flat hadn't been the first of his victims, apparently. Not ten minutes earlier, he'd thrown a pint of beer over a young female in the garden of The Lord Nelson. The girl's boyfriend had remonstrated with him and received a cut lip for his sins. The complaint had come in from the landlord, but with one thing and another had only just been picked up and passed on.

'So is he denying this one, then?' I asked an agitated McGovern. 'Case of mistaken identity, was it?'

According to McGovern, there was no doubt that Barford had been involved here, too. Like the second incident, his little happy slap had been snapped — and this time by numerous people. He'd be holding an exhibition at this rate, I mused.

'It's not that he's denying,' McGovern said. 'But he's being very cagey about this.'

He snatched up a clear plastic holder from his desk and waved the glinting contents before my eyes, for all the world like a hypnotist about to put a member of his audience in a trance.

'Exhibit A,' he said dramatically. 'A gold chain belonging to Annelise Parker, as identified by her best friend less than an hour ago and found on the person of Barford.'

I gave a low whistle.

'I want you to find out exactly where he was when that girl was drowned,' McGovern said. 'From where I'm standing, it doesn't look too good for him.'

I hated agreeing with McGovern, but this time I had to. It certainly looked as if Barford was intent on taking a personal vendetta on anyone his own age who happened to be born with a few more advantages than himself. He was a nasty piece of work, there was no denying it. I'd had a few brushes with him myself, so I could vouch for his nastiness personally. But murder?

* * *

'I don't know what you're fitting me up for this time, but I'll tell you again. I found this chain on the beach this morning,' said Barford.

He had his solicitor with him this time. A world-weary man in his forties, who gave off an odour of tobacco and defeat. The shoulders of his shiny navy jacket were liberally sprinkled with dandruff.

Patiently, he explained that I really had nothing on his client apart from a solitary gold chain that he'd more than amply accounted for.

'It's no secret that my client practises a bit of beachcombing on the off-chance he might rake up money or lost valuables. He just got lucky this time,' he said wearily.

'Yeah,' Barford joined in. 'I know you

think I had something to do with that girl what was washed up, but I never, see. I'm not saying I didn't do them other things, but I'd had a few. And they was giving it all that.'

He made a gesture with the fingers of his right hand to suggest a person speaking too much and mimicked the well-modulated accent of his victims — not very successfully, admittedly.

'You can't just take a swipe at people because you don't like the way they talk, Liam,' I sighed.

We were going round in circles here. Liam was giving me nothing I didn't already know. It was time to show him Annelise's photo.

'For the benefit of the tape, I am showing Mr Barford a photograph of the drowned girl, Annelise Parker,' I said.

Barford's solicitor began to shuffle his papers.

'This is preposterous!' he exclaimed. 'We're here to answer allegations of assault. My client has never set eyes on this young woman.'

'No, but hold up, I have!' Barford said.

The solicitor groaned and ran his fingers through his thinning hair. Dandruff rained down like confetti at a wedding.

Barford fixed his eyes on the photograph as he explained.

'She was at the pub, weren't she?' he said. 'I saw her when I came out the Gents. Standing outside the Ladies she was. Sobbing her eyes out.'

I stiffened. This sounded really interesting.

'Did you say anything to her?' I asked him.

He appeared to rack his brain. 'Yeah, I did, as it goes. Told her I'd buy her a drink if it'd make her feel better.'

As chat-up lines went, this wasn't the worst I'd heard.

'And how did she reply?'

'Said it was very kind of me, but that she didn't drink. Not these days. She had to look after herself, she said. So I said I was sorry to hear that and went back outside to the garden.'

Where he promptly tipped a pint of beer over some unsuspecting girl's head and cuffed her poor boyfriend in the mouth when he objected. Not good. But not murder.

And then I felt my pulse begin to race. Something Linus Golf-Whitham had said was playing on my memory. She'd been drinking, he'd insisted. You know what lightweights girls are, he'd said. But what had she said to Barford? That she didn't drink. Not these days.

Something else was pricking my mind. I looked down at the photograph. In the pub, I definitely remembered thinking I recognised the girl from somewhere. But then I'd brushed the thought aside. Leggy blondes with tans and bare midriffs were two a penny in Brockhaven in the summer, more was the pity, I'd mused.

But now Liam Barford's memory of Annelise Parker's words to him had triggered another memory. Was it really only Friday afternoon — two days ago — that I'd been held up for an appointment, because what I'd imagined would be a two-minute wait in the chemist's ended up being nearer a fifteen-minute one?

Think, girl, I told myself. This was

important. I had a good memory. A trained memory. Sometimes in the supermarket, when I was standing in a queue, I'd amuse myself by playing a solitaire version of the memory game we played at parties when I was a kid. But instead of remembering items on a tray, I'd try to memorise the details of people's shopping baskets.

And that's what I'd been doing as I stood behind the pretty blonde girl in the chemist's. Shower gel — two for one; a pack of hair bands; a tube of toothpaste; aftersun cream. And a pregnancy-testing kit.

With a swift movement of my arm that caused poor Liam Barford to duck, I switched off the tape with the words: 'Interview suspended at 2.02.'

'You're free to go, Mr Barford. Make sure you appear in court when you're summoned, that's all.'

★ ★ ★

'It really was the boyfriend's own fault. After all, we couldn't prove a thing. There were no prints on the dead body. Any scratches or bruising were par for the course. He just — came out and admitted it.'

'With a bit of encouragement from you, no doubt,' Dom said.

I smiled. 'It was just that word 'nag' that did it for me,' I explained to him.

We were strolling down the pier enjoying an ice-cream in the warm July sun.

'It's a word that jars with me, you see,' I continued.

'I imagine it's a word that jars with most women,' Dom said. 'And some men.'

'In the end, McGovern couldn't deny that Barford had nothing to do with the girl's drowning and that he was telling the truth about where he'd found the chain. He had to go along with the autopsy, too, when I told him what I'd found out about the girl's condition.'

'Not to mention her drinking habits,' Dom added.

'Yeah, I'm a bit annoyed with myself about that,' I said. 'I should have noticed she was only drinking tomato juice.'

Dom sighed. 'D'you never have a day off, Casey?' he said.

I shrugged. We were having a nice day. Why spoil it with the 'I am what I am and if you don't like it then you know what you can do' routine?

Dom obviously thought the same. What he said next was designed to flatter me and skirt us away from dangerous ground, I was certain of that.

'Your boss is a man's man,' he said. 'Not to mention a snob. He'd have been satisfied to take a gentleman's word at face value. They went for a swim. She got out of her depth. End of. Commiserations. And, of course, you knew nothing about the fact that your girlfriend was carrying your child, sir.'

I grinned up at Dom. It was a remarkably good impression of McGovern.

'How did you get him to confess that he'd deliberately led her out of her depth, pushed her head underwater and kept it there till she was dead?' he asked.

'I reminded him about Thursday night,' I said.

Dom furrowed his brow. 'Trouble outside your flat? Kids rowing. You told me,' he said. 'Was that them?' 'Brockhaven's a small place, even in summer. Although I admit it was only after I'd got him to raise his voice in protest that I realised it wasn't the first time I'd heard him getting angry with a lady.'

Dom gave a low whistle.

'It was a warm night. I had my bedroom window open. They were rowing. Hammer and tongs. I heard every word. That's what I told him,' I said.

Dom slowed to a standstill and turned to face me, his mouth slackening in disbelief. 'But your bedroom window looks out over your backyard,' he said. 'You couldn't possibly have heard what they were saying.'

'I know,' I said. 'But Linus Goff-Whitham didn't know that, did he?'

'So he fell for it?'

'Trouble with all that public-school education is that it's not necessarily as good as it's cracked up to be,' I said.

Dom chuckled. I happened to know he'd been to public school himself. And

Cambridge. Although he did his best to disguise it.

'You've got the cheek of the devil, Casey Clunes,' Dom said.

'I take it that's a compliment?' I said.

'Absolutely.'

There was a look of puppyish admiration on his face, which really wasn't a good look in a grown man. I was going to have to tell him sooner or later.

Things Bad Begun

1

It was rare for Casey Clunes to give in to feelings of despair over the amount of paperwork that came her way. As a rule, she dealt with it quietly and efficiently — unlike most of her male counterparts who delegated it to anyone unfortunate enough to be passing at the time — and then she got on with the part of the job she loved the most: solving crimes.

But now she sat in front of her computer as if frozen, the report she'd promised to finish writing by noon today not even begun. It was the only thing that stood between her and the three o'clock train to Cambridge. What on earth had made her agree to Dom's suggestion of this weekend reunion in Cambridge with two of his oldest friends from his student days?

Dom had been thrilled when he'd received an e-mail from Simon Pike to say how much he'd enjoyed a piece Dom had written and how delighted he was to have an old friend working for such a prestigious newspaper these days. According to Dom, Simon was nothing less than a genius; she knew it meant a lot to him that someone he admired so much had taken the trouble to write. Dom had e-mailed back immediately and out of this the invitation had arisen. Casey only wished Dom had asked her opinion before accepting for her, too.

'You'll love them both,' he had assured her. 'And they'll love you.'

Simon and his wife Imogen had both been first in their year — friendly rivals, apparently. And as if a couple of Firsts between them wasn't enough, they also had a PhD apiece. On top of that, there was the three-year-old daughter they'd cleverly produced along the way. Was there anything these two couldn't turn their minds to?

What would she find to talk about with either Simon or Imogen Pike for an entire weekend? Casey Clunes — who'd left school at sixteen and gone straight into the force, and who preferred her classics served up in bite-sized doses on the BBC, with a bag of crisps and a bottle of beer on the side. It wasn't as if she could do kiddie talk, either!

In the end, she managed to finish her report with time to kill. She could have left the station there and then and been in plenty of time for her train. But then, an hour before she was due to leave, she suddenly took it upon herself to chase up every detail of every case she was working on at the moment. It wouldn't have taken Freud to work out that it was simply a diversionary ploy.

'Casey, we'll manage,' DC Jane Rose insisted, when Casey had barged into her colleague's office, just to check on one more thing. 'Anybody would think you didn't trust us to work on our own. Surely you can manage two days away from the office.'

The thought suddenly occurred to Casey — what exactly was she in denial about? What was the real reason she didn't think she'd hit it off with Imogen and Simon Pike?

'You're jealous, Clunes,' she told

herself, as she picked up her weekend case and threw it into the back of the cab that had arrived to take her to the station. 'That's the long and the short of it. You've got a great big chip on your shoulder, because they went to Cambridge and the only place you went to is Hendon to do your basic training.' There now, she'd faced it. But it didn't make her feel any better.

She'd never been one to believe in destiny, but it seemed she was destined to get this train. Her very last attempt to escape her fate — by joining a queue of travellers to buy a coffee for the journey — failed miserably. She'd still managed to board with seconds to spare. Now she was struggling to remove the lid of her cup, which was proving quite a challenge.

'You be careful not to scald yourself, honey!'

Casey smiled at the older woman opposite. Even if she hadn't spoken, Casey would have picked her out immediately as American. There was a youthful vigour about her and her style of casual, brightly coloured dress screamed Middle America. With one final attempt she managed to prise off the lid at last.

'Maybe I should have stuck to bottled water.' She grimaced at the first sip.

The old lady leaned forward.

'I know it's a cliché and maybe I shouldn't say it, but one thing I miss about the States is they do know how to make a decent cup of coffee,' she said, with a wistful sigh.

Casey smiled. 'How long have you been over here?'

'Just a few weeks,' she said. 'I've been travelling. You know what we Americans are like. And visiting my son here in Brockhaven.'

'Nice,' Casey said. 'Is he settled in the UK?'

'Honey, he's as British as you are,' she said. 'He even drinks warm beer. My name's Arlene, by the way. Arlene Fanshaw. The Reverend Arlene Fanshaw, actually.'

Casey gulped. 'A reverend?'

The Reverend Fanshaw smiled at her. 'It's OK. I promise not to mention God.'

Casey felt awkward for a moment. To cover this up she owned up to her own profession.

'Between us we could empty a room in no time,' Arlene quipped.

For the rest of the journey they made the usual small talk of wayfaring strangers. Arlene, apparently, had once, many years ago, been a visiting scholar at one of the colleges and it was with a friend from those far-off halcyon days, as she described them, that she'd be spending the next week.

'I know my good friend, Eleanor, will have organised a deal of treats. She always does,' Arlene said, gathering her things together as the train began to slow down as they neared Cambridge. 'A trip to London, for sure. And then a Shakespeare here in Cambridge. It's the Festival, you know. Shakespeare in my old college gardens. Wonderful!'

'Mmm,' Casey replied non-committally, hauling her weekend bag down from the rack above her head. There were worse ways to spend your Saturday evenings, she supposed, but she couldn't think of many.

The train ground to a standstill and the doors opened, disgorging all the passengers. An extremely sprightly Arlene immediately disappeared into the throng. Casey made her way outside at a more leisurely pace.

No one was there to meet her but she hadn't expected it. It would have been nice to have been able to co-ordinate trains, so that she and Dom could have turned up at the Pikes' together as a couple, but, thanks to the complications of rail timetabling, that had proved impossible. Once inside the terraced house in Newnham that was the Pikes' home, it was clear from the two bottles of wine already empty that the party had started without her.

After the initial flurry of introductions, and the glass of wine that had been thrust into her hand, Casey — doing her best not to appear flustered by Simon's effusive air-kissing — sat down next to Dom in as close a proximity as propriety allowed and made the decision that if this was his friend, then he was going to be her friend, too. Imogen, Simon said, was out of the room, bathing Astrid, but she'd be down in a minute.

'Imo can't wait to meet you, Casey,' he said, finally taking a seat himself. 'We never ever imagined old Dom here would bag a girl in your line of business. Bit of a Lefty back in the old days, weren't you, mate?'

Dom mumbled something into his glass. Casey's resolution to like Simon just because he was Dom's friend was already dangling by a thread. It seemed to her that he was baiting her, thinly disguising his views about the police with a veneer of bonhomie. That wasn't a smile on his face, it was a sneer.

It was a relief when Imogen appeared, carrying a serious-faced, dark-haired child with her thumb in her mouth, wrapped in a big white towel.

'Are you the police lady?' the little girl said.

'You must be Astrid,' Casey replied with a smile.

'Where's your uniform?' Astrid countered, doing away with pleasantries and cutting right to the chase.

'I haven't got a uniform because I'm a detective.'

'That's *much* more important than an ordinary policeman, darling,' Simon said, taking his daughter from the arms of his wife.

'That's right,' Casey said with a gracious smile. 'Very much more important. I'll show you my identification, if you like.'

'You can read Burglar Bill to me,' Astrid said, handing the card back. 'When I'm in my Jim-Jams.'

'It'll be a pleasure,' Casey replied. It was odd, but she couldn't help feeling flattered that Astrid had picked her out as the person she wanted to read her bedtime story.

'She must like you,' Imogen said, as later, supper eaten and Astrid safely tucked up in bed, the four lounged in the living room, drinking coffee.

'She's delightful,' Casey said.

'What about you two?' Simon asked. He was taking up most of the settee now, while Imogen perched on the edge of her seat next to him. 'Any sign of the patter of tiny feet yet?'

'Simon!' Imogen sent him a chilly glare. It occurred to Casey that, though she obviously put up with a lot from Simon, there were limits.

'Whoops! Put my foot in it, have I?' Simon said. 'Me and my big mouth.'

To Casey's relief, Imogen swiftly changed the subject.

'Do you like Shakespeare, Casey?' There was a pleading note to her question that gave Casey no other choice but to answer that yes, she was a big fan.

'Then you'll never guess what a treat we've got lined up for you tomorrow!'

★   ★   ★

'It's a lovely evening for it,' Imogen said, fanning herself with her programme. 'The college grounds are just perfect for *Macbeth* with all the trees and mounds and everything. You could almost believe you were up in Scotland somewhere.'

Simon was doing something pompous with a bottle of champagne and a white cloth. Casey looked around. She had to agree with Imogen — albeit reluctantly

— that the weather and the surroundings were perfect. It was already growing dark. In the distance stood St Crispin's college itself. Someone — a woman with silver hair — was seated by a window in a wing chair, sipping coffee, immersed in a newspaper — probably *The Times*, Casey conjectured. What did Simon call them? Fellows. Even the language of this place was archaic, she decided, turning her attention to the set. The play was about to begin.

'So, what do you think of it so far, Casey?'

It was the interval and they were queuing for mulled wine, a drink Casey detested for its cloying sweetness, but she was so unexpectedly enchanted with everything tonight that she took the glass from the waiter with a polite thank-you.

'MacDuff's pretty hot,' she said, her tongue very firmly in her cheek. 'Breeches and boots. Such a good look!'

'I just wonder which quarto they're doing,' Simon complained, sipping his drink. 'And they're chopping some of the best lines.'

'Coo-ee!'

Someone was pushing her way through the crowd to get to Casey. It was Arlene, with her friend, Eleanor, Casey assumed.

'What are these so withered and so wild in their attire?' Simon muttered into his drink, as they approached.

Casey, ignoring him, greeted Arlene like an old friend. What a coincidence, they all agreed. But then Cambridge was like that, Arlene's friend said. Everyone knew everyone else. They chatted until the interval ended when they all went their separate ways back to their places.

Now it was pitch dark, the only light being artificial and that centred on the actors. Imogen had done well to bring the mosquito spray, which went up and down the row between the four of them as the drama played out.

Casey had never really 'got' Shakespeare at school, but now, in the dark, on a warm night in Cambridge, she was transported to the blasted heath of *Macbeth*'s drama.

When it was all over, the audience applauded rapturously, even Simon, Casey noticed, though that may have been the mellowing effect of the champagne, she figured.

She was leaning towards Dom to catch something he was saying above the applause, so she didn't notice it at first. The shadowy outline of a figure, a woman — distraught — waving her hands and stumbling in the dark, suddenly burst into the spotlight, scattering the startled actors as they gave their final bow.

'There's been a murder!' the woman cried. 'Oh, God! Someone call the police!'

* * *

'You've done well to keep this lot inside the grounds single-handedly.'

The DI, who'd introduced himself as John Madreld, spoke grudgingly.

Casey replied that she was a police officer — and police officers, as she was sure he'd agree, were never off duty.

John Madreld was a seriously over-weight man, whose forehead glistened with sweat on this humid summer night. 'We'll have to interview everybody, of course, in case they saw anything,' he sighed.

'I'd be willing to help,' Casey offered. The poor fellow clearly needed all the help he could get.

'Oh, that won't be necessary. My men have got it covered.'

Casey noticed at least two WPCs already busy with their notepads, talking to members of the public. John Madreld must have been on leave when the political correctness course had been running.

Simon, who had been listening in all this time, huffing and puffing, gave her an impatient nudge.

'Casey, we could be here for hours. Have you any idea how much babysitters charge after midnight?'

'Are you suggesting that you and Imogen should take priority?' If it had been up to her, she'd have left his interview till last just through spite, but John Madreld, surprisingly, came to Simon's rescue.

'Did you notice anything, sir?' he asked him.

'Of course not. I was glued to the performance.'

'And your wife, sir? Did she see anything?'

'Don't you think you ought to ask her?' Casey said.

John Madreld looked at his watch. Either he had a hot date or there was something he wanted to watch on late-night TV. Casey guessed the second thing.

'Oh, come on, Casey,' a clearly irritated Simon said. 'Imogen was sitting right next to me. She'd have said if she'd noticed anything.'

Turning to John Madreld, he said, 'Please, Inspector. If you're done with us, my wife and I would be very grateful if you'd allow us both to go home and drop our babysitter off.'

'Oh, I'm satisfied we don't need to detain you or your wife any longer, sir,' Madreld said.

Casey restrained a gasp of disbelief. This was lazy policing in the extreme. It was a relief when she heard her name called behind her and felt a hand on her arm.

'Officer,' she said, to the earnest-faced young woman who'd approached her. 'How can I help?'

'There are two older ladies sitting over there,' she said. 'Both quite distressed. One of them says she knows you.' She glanced down at her notebook. 'The Reverend Arlene Fanshaw? American lady?'

'We travelled to Cambridge together,' Casey said. 'She's staying with her friend, Eleanor.'

'Humphreys,' the WPC said, furnishing Casey with the surname that had been on the tip of her tongue. 'I've interviewed them and they're free to go. But in view of their distress . . . '

'You want me to accompany them home,' she said. 'Of course.'

She would have loved to stay and see the victim, already reported as being the very same woman she had noticed earlier through one of the college windows, sipping her coffee and reading her paper. She longed to interview the witness who'd found her, too, and to speak to the forensic officers, now making their way inside the college building to begin their work, but this was not her case. But by getting in a cab with Arlene and Eleanor, she'd at least be doing something useful.

Eleanor didn't live all that far away from St Crispin's — just over one of the two hills the city on the edge of the Fens boasted, in fact — and under normal circumstances she'd have walked home from town, she said, gratefully accepting the brandy that Dom held out to her, back in her own book-lined sitting room.

Casey believed her. Both Eleanor and Arlene were of that generation of brisk women whose motto was to soldier on under any circumstances — she admired them for it and hoped that at their age, she'd adopt the exact same point of view.

It was obvious from the way they followed Dom around the room that both women had fallen for him, and it was utterly understandable why. It had been Dom who'd summoned the taxi, helped both women into and out of it and taken Eleanor's key from her shaking hand to let them all inside her house.

'I knew her, you see,' a quickly fortified

Eleanor said. 'The victim, I mean.'

'We both did,' Arlene chimed in. 'Eudora Spencer was her name. We were at college together.'

'You were only at college with her for two terms,' Eleanor said, turning to her friend to correct her. Then, addressing Casey and Dom again, she added, 'Arlene was a visiting American scholar, you see. They came and went.'

'I knew her long enough.' It was clear from the way Arlene bristled as she spoke that she thought she had just as much right as her friend to be affected by the death of their mutual acquaintance.

'There may even be one or two photos of her as a young woman somewhere on these very walls,' Eleanor said, scanning the room. 'Yes, there! Just above that bookcase. And over on the other wall, next to the painting of King's Arlene gave me.'

Both photos were black and white and in both Eudora Spencer wore the same expression. Straight-backed, she smiled stiffly at the camera, in the way people unfamiliar with being snapped used to do. In one photo, in which she wore an evening gown, she stood as tall as the young man at her side. The other photo showed her towering over most of the other young women in the line-up who — much more casually dressed this time — were pictured with her. Which girl was Eleanor, she wondered, and what about Arlene? Was she there too?

'Who's the heart throb?' she asked.

Eleanor, flushed from her brandy, giggled girlishly, casting a glance in Arlene's direction. Something in their swift exchange convinced Casey there was a story to tell here.

'Will you tell her or shall I, Arlene?'

Arlene, who still hadn't touched a drop of her brandy, crossed her elegant legs and stared down at her lap.

'Honey,' she said, 'it's an old scandal. I'm sure Casey and her young man would rather be on their way home. It's awful late.'

But the temptation to revisit the past was too much for Eleanor in the end. 'Eudora Spencer came from a long line of Crispies,' she began.

Her father had been a Nobel Prize-winner and her mother had been a formidable philosopher, Eleanor went on to say. As an undergraduate, she — like most of the others in her crowd, Arlene included — had been in awe of Eudora, who was on first-name terms with the Vice-Chancellor and whose sherry parties were attended by some of the finest minds in Cambridge.

It had caused quite a stir when — from right under the nose of another girl — Eudora had walked off with her fiancé.

'Rufus Grainger,' Arlene butted in. 'Smart — smarter even than she was, folk said.'

'Oh, no, Arlene. They may have *said* that. But that was the Fifties, when people refused to believe a woman could be brighter than a man even with the evidence staring them in the face.' The glance she threw Casey was one of sympathetic sisterhood.

'Honey, I bow to your greater wisdom,' Arlene said. 'After all, I just *came* and went.'

Touché, Arlene! You go, girl! It

fascinated Casey just how this friendship had managed to survive as long as it had with all the sparring going on.

'So where's this — Rufus Grainger now?'

'Oh, he's been off the scene for years,' Eleanor said. 'Didn't last long, that marriage.'

'Is he in Cambridge still?'

Eleanor shrugged. All she'd heard was that he'd walked out one morning and never come back. As for Margaret — the girl he'd thrown over for Eudora — she'd left Cambridge without even graduating, poor thing. She'd been in a nursing home for years. A sad end to a sad life.

It was still warm, even though it was nearer to two o'clock than one, and when Dom had suggested walking back to Newnham instead of calling for a taxi, Casey had jumped at the chance to have some time alone with him.

'Bit of a busman's holiday this,' Dom said, 'for both of us.'

'The worst thing, though, is I've got to go home tomorrow and I won't get to know any more about this murder than your average Jo.'

Dom stopped walking, pulled her towards him and kissed her deeply.

'Thanks for trying to take my mind off it,' she said, when the kiss finally came to an end.

They continued their walk along The Backs. King's College, ethereal in the early summer dawn, made her feel like she was on a film set.

'I'm sorry about Simon,' Dom said, after a while.

'Don't be.' Casey didn't want to spoil her contented mood by bickering about Dom's friend.

'He's changed,' Dom said.

'Or maybe you have. Simon was the big cheese in your year, but look at you now. Writing stunning articles for a top-notch London newspaper. And what's he doing? Teaching undergraduates for a pittance, yet carrying on as if he's God's gift to education. Imogen must have the patience of a saint,' she added.

'It's like she's forgotten she ever had a brain,' he said. 'I blame motherhood. Have you noticed how she seems to opt out of every discussion and more or less let Simon speak for both of them?'

'She's often busy with Astrid, remember,' Casey said, in Imogen's defence.

'You're right. Astrid seems to have become her main focus these days,' Dom agreed.

'Is that a bad thing? She's only three, after all,' Casey reminded him.

She couldn't have explained why, but Dom's words touched a nerve. Since meeting Astrid, she'd caught herself thinking that maybe motherhood wasn't as dreadful a condition as she'd once, long ago, made up her mind it was. Somewhere in the distance a clock chimed. She couldn't decide if it were a real one or if, in fact, it was the ominous ticking of that biological one she'd read so much about.

2

Next morning, Casey flicked through all the TV channels, hoping for some in-depth reportage of the Cambridge murder, but it soon became apparent that it was far too early in the investigation for any more than the salient facts to be released.

That lunch-time, Simon drove them all out to Madingley, where Astrid exhausted herself on the swings and charmed everyone watching her. Casey's train was due to leave at four, but before she left she'd already made up her mind to ring John Madreld to see if he had any news.

'It looks like we've got a suspect,' Madreld said, over the phone. 'One Francis Challenger. Scene-shifter, with the occasional walk-on part, with the touring company that performed last night. Somehow managed to escape the cordon you threw.'

Casey swore colourfully and apologised

if she'd done anything to jeopardise the investigation. Madreld assured her she'd done more than anybody could have expected, considering she was meant to be having a night off. If it had been him, he said, he'd never have owned up to being a copper. Casey believed him, having witnessed his slipshod methods the night before.

This Francis Challenger had form — and plenty of it, even though he was barely twenty-one, Madreld said. It was while he was doing his last stretch, apparently, that he'd shown such enthusiasm in the drama classes some of the members of the company put on for the prison inmates.

'Out of the goodness of their hearts,' Madreld remarked. 'Liberal loonies.'

'What about the murder weapon?'

There'd been enough swords to cut a swathe through the entire audience last night. Not to mention the infamous dagger.

'Nasty,' Madreld said. 'A skewer. About six inches in length, made of hardwood. You may have eaten a kebab or two off something similar.'

Casey shuddered. Either this killer was driven by fury or he was the type who lacked all traces of delicate feelings.

★ ★ ★

Madreld had promised to keep in touch with Casey about the outcome of the case, but later, as she dozed on the train, having parted from Dom at the station and said goodbye to the Pikes — not without some relief — she knew that if she wanted to be kept informed she was going to have to do all the running.

What a strange weekend it had turned out to be. It would be a relief to reach Brockhaven. It was Astrid's birthday soon and Casey's thoughts turned to what would be a suitable present for her. What had come over her? she wondered, catching herself off guard once more. A murder had been committed and here she was wondering what would make a suitable present for a girl about to be four, instead of pondering on the events of the night before. She was going to have to watch herself. What if she'd let down her guard already and Dom had spotted that maternal glint in her eye? No, surely it hadn't been *that* obvious.

Arriving at Brockhaven, she decided to stop off at the police station to see if she'd missed anything. She had. The body of an old tramp had been discovered just hours ago, at the foot of the multi-storey car park.

'Did he jump or was he pushed?' Casey asked, as she watched her colleague Jane carefully bag up the contents of the dead man's pockets.

'We won't know for a week, at least,' Jane sighed. 'A dead tramp's hardly priority as far as the budget's concerned, unfortunately.'

'Sad, but true,' Casey agreed. 'Let's have a look at that photo before you bag it.'

Jane handed it over. The photo was black and white and showed a young, good-looking man in a DJ, standing next to a young woman in an evening gown.

Casey gasped, her eyes riveted on the photo.

'What's the matter, Casey? You're shaking!' Jane exclaimed.

'This man,' Casey said, doing her best to keep her voice steady. 'I can identify him. His name is Rufus Grainger and last night his wife was murdered in the gardens of St Crispin's College.'

★   ★   ★

'I think I've got something for you.'

Casey — in a hurry to tell him of the possible lead that she'd discovered — had been waiting to be put through to Inspector John Madreld for so long that her patience had all but evaporated. Now that he'd finally been located, she just wanted to get her story out. But now he was obstructing her at every turn.

Was she still in Cambridge? Hadn't she gone back to wherever it was she'd come from in the first place? What did she mean by *lead*? He sincerely hoped she wasn't treading on his patch, because it would be very much frowned on by his superiors if that was the case.

John Madreld was a man who clearly

needed his ego massaging, Casey decided. No, she wasn't trying to interfere in a case she had no doubts he was perfectly capable of solving standing on his head. And no she wasn't still in Cambridge but back in Brockhaven — nice, little seaside town, actually, hadn't he heard of it? And, fair enough, her information might not be a lead exactly, but it might be of some help.

She hoped she sounded more courteous than he did when, with a weary sigh, he told her she might as well tell him what she had. Briefly, she told him about the body that had been found at the foot of the multi-storey car park in Brockhaven, which they'd initially assumed to belong to an old tramp, but which now appeared to belong to Rufus Grainger, Eudora Spencer's husband. A strange coincidence, didn't he agree? She wondered if Madreld wanted to come to Brockhaven and have a look at this latest body for himself.

'We might be able to piece together any connection there may be between this death and the first one, if we put our heads together,' she suggested.

Madreld declined. 'Keep me in the loop,' he said, 'but I'm not sure the discovery of this second body merits a car journey.'

Madreld was playing his cards extremely close to his chest. He must have more on this Challenger boy than he was letting on. Well, if he wouldn't give anything away she was going to have to ask him.

'What about Francis Challenger? Have you got anything on him?'

'Nothing,' came the short reply.

She didn't believe a word of it. 'Any news of his whereabouts?' she persisted.

'Took off right after the murder. Went back to his digs, cleared his stuff out and hasn't been seen since.'

'You're sure he's done it, aren't you?' she said.

'Maybe he has, maybe he hasn't.'

Taking a deep breath, Casey steamrollered on. Had Madreld considered, for example, that Challenger had only legged it so soon after the murder because, as someone with a criminal record, he knew he'd be number-one suspect? What if it had been Rufus Grainger, not Challenger who'd murdered Professor Spencer, then returned to Brockhaven and, in a fit of remorse, committed suicide over his crime? There was a third option, too. Everyone was assuming Grainger's death had been a suicide. But what if everyone was wrong and the murderer of Eudora Spencer had been Grainger's murderer, too?

'You've got some interesting ideas, Inspector Clunes,' Madreld said. 'I'll bear them in mind in my investigation. But now, if you'll excuse me, there's somewhere I've got to be.'

'Of course, Inspector Madreld,' Casey said stiffly.

Casey glared at the phone's receiver in her hand. However remote the link between Eudora Spencer, Rufus Grainger and Francis Challenger, surely it was Madreld's job to pursue it? Clearly he didn't think so. But if Madreld wasn't interested in finding the answers to these questions then she was. Between exchanging goodbyes and putting the phone down, her decision to revisit the scene of the crime had somehow made itself.

Her first stop was St Crispin's College, elegantly bathed in glorious, high-summer sunshine. Casey had driven down this time, and it was a relief to get out of her car after a tediously slow and sticky journey.

She couldn't believe how easy it had been to get past the Porter's Lodge with just a flash of her ID card. It had taken only a phone call to ascertain that Jenny, the woman who'd discovered the body of Eudora Spencer, was down in the Old Kitchen and would be pleased to speak to her.

She'd declined to be accompanied there and had easily found her way herself. Jenny Bates, a sprightly woman in her sixties, was waiting for her. She expressed surprise that she was being interviewed again.

'It'll be about Professor Spencer's visitor, like I told that other police Inspector,' she said. 'That Francis Challenger one. Him with his picture all over the *Cambridge Evening News*.'

Casey gave a start. She'd spoken to John Madreld less than four hours ago, just before she'd got into her car to drive back to Cambridge. It would have cost him nothing to pass on the information that Challenger wasn't a stranger to Eudora Spencer, surely? Why couldn't he have said there was no need for him to come down to Brockhaven and look at the body of Rufus Grainger because his evidence against Challenger was incontrovertible, instead of all that hedging — not to mention downright stonewalling?

'We can't go over to the SCR because it's a crime scene, as you'll know,' Jenny said, gesturing to a chair at the massive, scrubbed pine table that took pride of place in the kitchen.

Pulling up another chair for herself, Jenny Bates sat down and mopped her brow with a tissue she'd retrieved from the pocket of the white nylon overall she was wearing — hardly the ideal garb for temperatures in the high seventies.

The SCR had been where the body of Eudora Spencer had been found. Casey knew from Dom that the initials stood for Senior Common Room. She'd learned other quaint Cambridge expressions from him, too, in the time she'd known him. For example, that students 'came up' at the beginning of term and 'went down' at the end of term, unless of course they were 'sent down', in which case they were never allowed to 'come up' ever again.

'I thought he was a wrong 'un as soon as I clapped eyes on him,' Jenny said, folding her thin, careworn hands in front of her. 'That's why I insisted on being there when he spoke to her, just in case there was any trouble.'

He'd been researching his family tree, she said, and he'd told Professor Spencer that he'd got as far as his grandparents.

''Course, she snatched at this as a brilliant opportunity to put him down. Told him he hadn't got very far, didn't she? Typical of her, that was.' Jenny sniffed.

The boy hadn't liked being talked down to one bit, she said. She felt guilty at saying it under the circumstances, Jenny confided, but she'd almost felt sorry for him then.

'Professor Spencer was the insensitive

type,' she said. 'To give her the benefit of the doubt, you could say it was because she had her mind on higher matters.'

It was clear to Casey that that wasn't her interpretation of Eudora Spencer's lack of feeling.

The boy was flustered by her words, she went on to say, like he knew Professor Spencer thought he was stupid and it really mattered to him that she didn't. But when he'd announced his grandfather's name, the boot was on the other foot.

'It was her that was flustered this time,' Jenny said triumphantly. 'My grandfather's name is Rufus Grainger, he said. So you must be my grandmother.'

Jenny shook her head at the absurdity of it, a wry smile on her face. 'She went grey. It was a good job that she was sitting down or else she'd have fallen down, I reckon.'

'She was shocked, then?' Casey said. 'Did she say anything?'

'Told him to get out,' Jenny replied. 'Said it was impossible for her to be his grandmother being as how she'd never even had any children. He was shaking, waving this bit of paper in her face, telling her her husband's name was on it next to hers, so it had to be.' Jenny fanned herself frantically. It was as if even the memory of this heated discussion had raised her temperature. 'I had to tell him to go, too. But he wouldn't budge. 'I've come for some answers,' he said, 'and I won't go till I get them.' I tell you, I was scared, even if she wasn't.'

It came as no surprise to Casey at all that a woman like Eudora Spencer wouldn't take kindly to threats. She was made from the same mould as her two college classmates, Arlene and Eleanor, whom Casey believed would be equally adept at standing up to any aggression. But she'd clearly been shaken — and who wouldn't be on learning they had a grandson they'd never till that moment clapped eyes on before?

Eudora Spencer had firmly denied having ever had any children. Was she lying or was she telling the truth? If she'd been telling the truth, then why would she have appeared so agitated by the

112

boy's claim that she was his long-lost granny? And if she was lying, then why? She'd married her husband on graduation — if she'd had a child old enough to be Challenger's father, then that child would have been born in wedlock. So where was the scandal? Unless, of course, the son had been born to Rufus Grainger and another woman altogether.

'Did he get any answers?' Casey asked.

'Can't say if he did or if he didn't,' Jenny said. 'She muttered a name. Margaret somebody — my hearing's not as good as it was, I'm afraid, Officer.'

The name rang a bell. Wasn't she the girl to whom Rufus Grainger had once been engaged, before Eudora muscled in? So it was the matter of a baby that had led to her leaving university and never returning. What a shock it must have been for her to see the son of Rufus's love child in the flesh.

'She said she had no address for her, but she wrote someone else's address down and gave it to him,' Jenny said.

'Did she say who?'

'Something about a woman she'd been

113

an undergraduate with years ago.' She shook her head sorrowfully at her inability to remember the woman's name. 'I do remember the Prof saying that she still lived in Cambridge and she might know the whereabouts of this Margaret woman, though,' she added, in mitigation.

Was Eleanor Humphreys the name she'd given this Francis Challenger? Madreld would have followed it up by now. She might as well go back to Brockhaven and sort out the crime on her own patch, instead of meddling where she wasn't wanted.

'Well, Jenny,' she said, as she stood to take her leave. 'You've been very helpful.'

Jenny shook her head. 'I'm afraid I haven't, Inspector,' she said. 'And I have to admit it fair gives me a turn every time I think of that Francis Challenger being on the loose.'

Casey offered Jenny her hand to shake.

'The police are on the look out for him all over the country, Jenny,' she said. 'They'll catch him, rest assured.'

'I wish that I had your confidence, Inspector,' Jenny said, waving goodbye.

Reluctantly she slid into the front seat of her car. She didn't fancy the return trip, that was for sure, but what possible reason could she give her superiors for staying in Cambridge any longer, given that John Madreld had made it perfectly clear there was no role for her in this case whatsoever? Scrabbling about in the glove compartment for the bottle of water she always kept there — which turned out to be lukewarm now — she switched on her car radio while pondering her next move.

'Suspected murderer Francis Challenger is still on the run more than thirty-six hours after the body of a female Cambridge Professor of Philosophy was discovered late Saturday evening. So far there appears to be no motive for the attack. Members of the public are warned not to approach him if they think they recognise him, but to call the police immediately.'

Challenger could be anywhere, if the news report was correct. Unless, of course, Madreld enjoyed playing just as fast and loose with the BBC and the British public as he clearly did with her.

Next came a traffic report.

'*The A14 and parts of the M11 have come to a complete standstill this morning after three separate accidents . . . '*

From the sound of it, she decided, her route home wasn't going to be passable any time soon. What to do in the meantime? She could kick around Cambridge for a while, but in this heat she'd just melt. What she would really like to do was to sit in someone's nice, shady garden, sipping ice-cold lemonade through a straw.

Any time you're in Cambridge, my dear, please do drop in. I'll be delighted to see you. Eleanor Humphreys wasn't the type to issue invitations she didn't mean. She'd like to tell her and Arlene about Rufus, too — he was a friend once, after all. At the Porter's Lodge she gave the porter a wave and turned right, in the direction of Eleanor's house. It looked like fate had dictated her next move.

But Casey was disappointed when it became clear, after several attempts at ringing the doorbell, that there was no one home. She wondered if Eleanor and

Arlene had chosen today to go off to London for a tour of the galleries, as they'd said they might. So what now? she wondered, glancing up and down the empty street.

The thought was taking root in her head that Arlene and Eleanor weren't the only people she knew in Cambridge. Removing her phone from her bag, she toyed with it for a while. She'd ring first, and ascertain if Simon was there and if he were then she'd say she was calling just to check the date of Astrid's birthday again. If he wasn't and Imogen invited her round, then she'd accept.

Thirty minutes later, Casey was sipping ice-cold lemonade through a straw just as she'd dreamed of doing earlier. Imogen commiserated with her about the problems on the road and even insisted on putting her up for the night, should she feel she really couldn't face the journey home. In fact, she said, she'd be glad of some adult company, since Simon was away on a conference overnight.

Casey agreed with alacrity. The news on her car radio on the way to Newnham had suggested there'd be no let up in traffic for hours yet. But, if Imogen didn't mind, she did want to try Eleanor's house again later. Sooner or later, the news of Rufus Grainger's death would be announced, now the marital connection between him and the Cambridge Professor had been discovered.

'I'd much prefer the two women to learn of his death from me and not from some newscaster,' she said. 'And I'd much rather deliver the news in person.'

It was agreed that Casey would drive back to Eleanor's house while Imogen was putting Astrid to bed and then the two of them could share a salad, a bottle of cold rosé and some grown-up conversation.

'It'll be fun,' Imogen said, refilling Casey's glass. 'Astrid's lovely, but sometimes I envy Simon, rushing off to catch a train to some place or other to swap stimulating ideas.'

Astrid, in sun hat, armbands and very little else, was happily splashing away in her pool, bucket and spade in hand.

'Actually, we just learned today that

118

Simon's got tenure at last,' Imogen said.

'Congratulations,' Casey murmured.

'It was what he'd been working towards for the last five years. What we were both working towards — once.' Her voice became subdued. 'But when Astrid came along I said goodbye to all that.'

Casey gazed over at Astrid, splashing and shrieking contentedly.

'We decided one of us should take a back seat for a while — till she's old enough to go to school,' Imogen added.

'You'll have your turn,' Casey said.

'It's going to be harder than I was led to believe, though,' Imogen sighed. 'You'd be surprised how little things have changed for women in my line of business.'

Astrid, suddenly deciding she'd had enough, clambered out of the water, and, dripping wet, ran down the garden to where Casey and Imogen were seated.

'Of course, your organisation is bound to be much more forward thinking,' she added, reaching for a towel to wrap her daughter in.

'I'm sure it is,' Casey said. She spoke

the words confidently, but, by contrast, her mood had taken a sudden unexpected dive.

Dusk was falling as Casey pulled up outside Eleanor's house for the second time that day. People were coming out to water their gardens now the air was cooler, but there was no sign of life from Eleanor's house. She should have got her number from the phone book and rung first before making this second trip, because it was clear from the curtains that were still closed that the two women hadn't yet returned.

Casey walked up Eleanor's path, rang the bell and waited. There was no reply so she tried again, glancing around at the flowers drooping from thirst in the border of Eleanor's pocket-handkerchief-sized front garden.

It was no use. She'd have to try again tomorrow. But this time she'd ring first. And then, as she turned to walk back to her car, a movement at the upstairs window caught her eye.

Quickly, Casey retraced her steps. She'd made a mistake. They were home after all. It was the heat, she decided. Exhausted after their day out, it was taking them a little longer to get to the door, that was all.

Once more she rang the bell, this time calling first Eleanor's name, then Arlene's, through the letter-box. Why weren't they answering? She could definitely hear movement from inside. Then someone coughed. Casey stiffened. Something wasn't right, she was sure of it. If neither Eleanor nor Arlene could get to the door there had to be a reason why. And then she heard it. A cry of fear, followed by the sounds of a scuffle and a slamming door.

3

Two minutes previously everything had been normal. Arlene had been wiping the dishes after lunch, feeling tetchy because she'd slept little last night due to the heat. Running through her head had been all sorts of stuff and nonsense about English houses — freezing cold in winter, baking hot in summer and how it always came as a surprise each time she returned to this country, though, heaven knows, she ought to be used to it by now. And now this. In the space of two minutes their cosy little world had turned upside down.

The intruder had slipped in through the wide-open French windows overlooking Eleanor's tiny paved back yard, fumbling them closed immediately behind him before clumsily drawing down the blind. Eleanor, with a shriek, had dropped a glass in surprise and was now on her hands and knees with a dustpan and brush. Arlene was still trying to steady herself at the sink, unwilling to give the young man any indication of how frightened she was.

'A bit of money and some food. That's all I want. Then I'll go,' he said.

He stood there, slim, hair untamed, blue jeans and T-shirt. Eleanor picked out the name *The Killers* on his chest. If there was a funny side to that, she wasn't seeing it right now. Crosswise over his shoulder he'd slung a putty-coloured canvas bag.

All his remarks so far he'd addressed to Eleanor — or rather to the back of Eleanor's head. Back and forth she went with the hand brush, till there was really nothing left to sweep up.

'You helped me last time. I just thought . . . '

Eleanor's repetitive sweeping slowed to a stop. At Arlene's puzzled gasp she raised her chin.

'What the hell's going on?' As a rule, Arlene didn't swear, but some things called for strong language just as some things called for strong drink. 'Didn't you think to tell me he'd been here before?'

She wanted to add that there was also

the small matter of informing the police but thought it wise at this stage to leave them out of it.

'I didn't want to worry you. Besides it was months ago — before any of this business with Eudora.'

Well, that was one way of putting it — *this business with Eudora*. Eudora had been murdered and more than likely by this young man. The entire British police force was after him.

For the first time, Francis Challenger seemed to realise there was another person in the room.

'She was good to me that time,' he said, glancing in her direction before turning back to Eleanor. 'Giving me my gran's address. I went to see her, you know.'

'That's nice.' Eleanor's voice was faint.

'I should have known her as my granny right away. She was sweet. Like a proper granny should be.' His expression hardened. 'Not like that other one. I'm glad I was wrong about her and she wasn't my grandmother at all.'

Arlene raised her eyebrows quizzically for explanation.

'Margaret Buckley,' Eleanor whispered. 'She had an illegitimate child, fifty years ago or more. Francis's mother. I was Eleanor's room-mate. When she left, she swore me to secrecy.'

'She never left — not of her own accord, that's for sure. That *bitch* drove her out. Got her a place in some hostel for unmarried posh girls who couldn't keep their babies.'

Arlene was doing her best to piece together all these bits of the story that between them Eleanor and Francis Challenger were telling her. She knew about Rupert and Margaret, of course, and she'd known how, when Eudora had fixed on Rupert, Margaret had simply left not only St Crispin's, but Cambridge too. She'd left herself a little while after, to return to the States, so for her the story had ceased to be of any interest.

But for Francis it lived on and now he'd drawn Eleanor and herself into the pages of its sequel. Margaret had been overjoyed to see him, he told them. She'd cried and cried, and hugged him tight and begged him to forgive her for everything bad she'd ever done to him. From the proud way he boasted of their encounter it was easy to see that affection was a novelty for Francis.

'It was never her fault,' Francis said. 'None of it. You *had* to give your baby away in those days. When she gave my mum away, she thought she'd go to a good home. She couldn't have known she'd go into care. Same as me.'

It was then he began to curse Eudora and, in a stream of disconnected language, he spewed out exactly how it was that she'd deserved to die. For making fun of him, so Arlene gathered, and for cutting him off from his grandparents, who could have helped him get somewhere in life. And then there were all the lives she'd ruined — three generations who could have known and loved each other.

'Look what she did to my grandfather.' His hand shook as he dug deep into his canvas bag and drew out a tattered envelope. 'I wrote to him, asked if we could meet. He was a tramp, thanks to her. A drunk. Did you know that?'

The hard edge to his voice caused Eleanor — on her feet at last — to cringe. It was as if the penny had just dropped with her and for the first time she had an inkling that Francis Challenger's mental state wasn't as stable as she'd imagined it to be. Eleanor, small-boned and frail as she'd become over the years, already looked like she might be at the end of her tether.

Arlene, on the contrary, stood her ground. She'd recognised the wild look in his eyes immediately. He was clearly a drug addict on the way down from a high. It was important to keep him calm and to keep calm themselves.

Francis put up no resistance when Arlene suggested going somewhere more comfortable. He was happy enough to accept the lemon barley water she offered him too and — with Eleanor — to trail after her into the living room. He was beginning to trust her, she was sure. The thing was to build on that trust, so that between them they could persuade him trying to run away was hopeless and the best thing would be to give himself up,

127

sooner rather than later.

'Let's sit down, shall we, Francis, and you can read your grandfather's letter to us,' she said, taking Eleanor gently by the arm and drawing her down next to her on to the settee. She immediately felt her friend's resolve stiffen and took courage from it.

But then, just as everything seemed set on going right, it changed in a moment. For Eleanor, the ring on the doorbell would have signified rescue and resolution. That could be the only reason, Arlene surmised, for her to blurt out that Francis must know he was a wanted man and it was time to stop his silly game right now.

When he pulled out the gun, which he now waved in their general direction, it wasn't fear she felt but fury. It was un-Christian of her but she couldn't help being mad with Eleanor. Couldn't she have predicted the effect her words would have on Francis, in his state of mind? Because of her carelessness, they'd gone from being almost trusted friends to dangerous enemies. And now, after whoever it was had given up on them and gone away, they were hostages.

'We're not going to shout for help, Francis. Promise. Are we, Eleanor?'

She nudged her friend, who nodded fervently. Arlene was relieved that Eleanor had apparently taken a vow of silence.

'You'd better not, if you know what's good for you.' He was shaking, but with fright or withdrawal symptoms, Arlene didn't know.

She wasn't beaten. She was just going to have to start again and rebuild his trust piece by piece. It would take time, but they had plenty of that. Surreptitiously, she glanced at the gun that Francis had placed on top of his canvas bag, in full view, no doubt as a reminder of how quickly he'd be able to retrieve it, should the need arise.

'You were reading us your letter,' she said, trying to encourage him with a smile.

'Better if you read it.'

He held it out and Arlene took it from him.

'I'm dyslexic,' he said, 'though I had to go to prison to get it diagnosed, didn't I?

'Course, if they'd bothered to measure my IQ against it when I was a kid they might have worked it out instead of throwing me in with all the troublemakers in the bottom set.' He laughed bitterly at the irony of this. 'But I was a kid from a care home, wasn't I? Like my mother and my father too, for all I knew. Why would they have bothered?'

The pitch of his voice rose up a notch. Eleanor's shoulder trembled faintly against her own.

'You were badly let down by everyone.' He seemed to calm down at this. 'Shall I read the letter now?' she said.

With a sharp nod of the head, he gave his assent. Arlene was relieved the bi-focal shades she'd been wearing for her trip to the market earlier still hung around her neck on a gilt chain. The prospect of trying Francis Challenger's patience with a half-hour hunt for her reading glasses was not a pleasant one. She began.

The envelope had been addressed, crossed out and re-addressed several times, but in the end it had reached its intended recipient at Target House, Brockhaven. To think, she'd been in Brockhaven herself only last week. What if Rufus Grainger had brushed by her without her even noticing? She felt uncomfortable at the thought of it. Isn't that what homeless people often told her in the course of her work with them — that 'normal' people just didn't see them? Then her thoughts turned briefly to Casey Clunes, that smart young woman she'd met — first on the train and subsequently on the night of Eudora's murder. What would she make of all this? she wondered.

Clearing her throat, she began. The letter was a long one. In it Rufus thanked his grandson for his letter and said how happy he was that he'd been united with his grandmother at long last. He was sorry for the treatment meted out to him by Eudora. She was a hard woman with a heart of stone, who'd never minded whom she trampled over to get what she wanted.

She looked up to see Francis, narrow-eyed, half-smiling, nodding in agreement with these words. Swallowing hard, she resumed her reading.

Imagine me as a young man, Francis. I came from nothing but I had brains and ambition. When I met Margaret I felt as if I'd come home. Like me, her background was working class and we gravitated towards each other.

Arlene took a breath. What was it with the British and their obsession with class? She loved England, but, honestly, at times they were such a snooty bunch. She read on.

We would have married. I'd have become a schoolteacher, perhaps, if I were lucky, rising to the rank of headmaster. She would have become the mother of my children. But even in the moment we became engaged I knew that this second-rate way of life was not for me. When Eudora — wealthy, well-connected, brilliant and beautiful — set her cap at me, I'm afraid I did what any young man with ambition would do. I allowed myself to be seduced.

Next to her Eleanor wriggled uncomfortably. Any talk of sex had that effect on her, Arlene remembered.

It was the biggest mistake of my life and one I'm still paying for.

That was quite a statement, Arlene mused. Francis had begun to pace up and down the tiny living room, gun in hand. It was starting to get on her nerves.

'Do you want me to go on?' she said, conscious she might sound snappy.

'No,' he said. 'I know the rest.'

Carefully, she put it back into the envelope but not before she'd taken in the salient points. She read how Eudora had insisted he break off ties with Margaret and any issue in return for the comfortable life she offered him — how he'd accepted but, full of guilt at this pact he'd made, turned to drink — how, one day, he'd simply walked out on Eudora, his lovely house, his Rolls-Royce and his summers in Tuscany and taken to the road.

'I can quote you the last sentence if you like,' Francis said.

'Not if it upsets you,' Arlene began, but already he was quoting, word for word, Rufus Grainger's apology for never having been a father to Francis's mother and never knowing his grandson either.

It's nice of you to offer to come here to visit me, but really, dear boy, I think it's far too late for me to get to know you now. All things considered, I have nothing to offer you.

Arlene saw herself as a liberal, with a small *l*. She worked with the poor and the disadvantaged and she knew all about the consequences of both. How different Francis Challenger's life would have turned out if Rufus and Eudora had acknowledged his mother, seen to it that the home she'd gone to was a caring, loving one — adopted her themselves even. With two such educated people watching over them, who knows how his life may have turned out?

Yet, such a view was too simplistic. Francis *had* been given another chance, if what she'd pieced together from interviews on TV and in the newspapers was to be believed.

The director of the touring theatre group in whose employ the young man had been at the time of Eudora's death had spoken with enthusiasm and at length about how his company had hoped, by taking drama inside penal institutions and running acting classes for the inmates, they might make a difference to their lives. One such inmate had been Francis Challenger, who'd shown great enthusiasm and some talent for acting. So much so that the director had made a promise to the young man that once he got out of prison after he'd served his time — his third conviction, apparently — there'd be a job waiting for him in the company.

He'd been given a chance at redemption and he'd blown it. It pained Arlene to think so badly of this poor misguided boy but the truth was that killing Eudora had been a wicked act, motivated by selfishness. A character flaw he shared with his grandfather, who — as the contents of his letter had revealed — was just as keen to lay the blame for his own weakness of character elsewhere as Francis was.

There was nothing to be done but sit it out. All afternoon they remained where they were, Francis alternately pacing then leaning up against a wall, talking about how hard his life had been and how differently it would have turned out if it hadn't been for Eudora Spencer. Meanwhile, Arlene, exhausted, sympathised while Eleanor wisely kept her vow of silence.

It was almost a relief when, later in the evening, as the sun set at the back of the house, the bell rang again. Eleanor, dozing, hadn't heard it, thank God, or who knew what madness may have ensued if she'd failed to keep control of her tongue?

She and Francis stiffened, panic assaulting them both.

'Get up,' he hissed.

Arlene obliged.

'Move. Up the stairs.'

Whoever it was had gone away; his panic was unreasonable. But then, reason had long ago stopped playing any part in Francis's decision-making process. Up the stairs he pushed her, digging the butt of the gun into her back. On the top step she stumbled. Flinging open the door of her bedroom, he pushed her inside and slammed the door behind her.

* * *

Casey hadn't wasted a moment in putting two and two together. Something was seriously amiss. This was the only house in the street with all the curtains and blinds drawn. Now, as the evening air grew tame after its earlier fierceness, every other house but this one had thrown open windows and doors to welcome in the balmy breeze.

And then there'd been that cry, the sound of stumbling, unless she'd been very much mistaken. Walking as sound-lessly away from the house as she could, she removed herself out of range of anyone inside who might pick up her voice. And then she made a phone call.

★ ★ ★

It was getting dark when Francis opened the door to the bedroom. She'd been lying there on the bed, dozing, her hands tied by a silk scarf Francis, rummaging through her drawer, had pulled out. There was no noise from downstairs and she prayed Eleanor was safe.

In fact, she realised, there was no noise anywhere. At this time of the evening there should be people walking past, cars, always cars, the chink of glasses as the neighbours took advantage of the last of the daylight to enjoy their barbecues or their *al fresco* suppers. But all she heard was the occasional burst of birdsong. How very strange.

'Francis.' Her voice came out as a croak.

'*I know,*' he spat out.

So he'd heard it too — the silence that could mean only one thing. *They were surrounded.* Whoever it was who'd called earlier had realised they were home but something was amiss and had called the police. One phone call had set the whole thing in motion. Out there were police officers, their guns trained on this house. Soon enough the phone would ring and someone would ask to speak to Francis. And then the long period of negotiating would begin.

All this she explained to Francis, quietly and patiently, as he sat at the end of her bed. When he began to cry she took the gun away from him and slid it under the bed, without him even noticing.

'I'll come and see you, Francis, when I can,' she said, taking him in her arms and holding him tight. 'You'll be OK this time.'

★ ★ ★

Dom had come up from London for the party, which Imogen had decided was to be a joint one for Arlene, Eleanor and Astrid — who technically wouldn't be

139

four for a couple of weeks, but since the weather was so good it was thought they ought to take advantage of it.

Arlene and Eleanor still hadn't tired of being feted and were at present holding court inside the house. Casey and Dom, surrounded by some half-dozen three-year-olds, were in the garden. They'd just organised a particularly successful game of musical chairs and had now been graciously let off the hook by Imogen, who said she'd ordered Simon to take over just as soon as he'd put some more champagne on ice.

'You two take some time for yourselves,' she said. 'You deserve it.'

They both flopped into deckchairs, but not before grabbing a glass of wine each.

'You've been in your element with all these kids,' Dom teased.

'Yeah, well, I enjoyed it.' She tried to sound restrained.

'Me too. They're a hoot at this age.'

Casey cast Dom a sidelong look. What was he really saying? she wondered. That, like her, he could see past the bump and the sick and the nappies too?

'Did you see the little girl with the stripey hair?'

'The one who thought the *huge* plate of cocktail sausages in front of her was just for her?'

'She ate every last one without even blinking. It was like she was involved in one of those eating competitions. Priceless!'

Dom was a great raconteur. Casey listened, with a nod here, a smile there and a grunt of agreement when it was required. Beneath the words he spoke were ones unspoken — the shadow of a thought that had pulsed into life when, like herself, he'd been looking the other way.

'Why are you looking at me like that?' Dom said. 'What have I said that's so funny?'

'Oh, nothing,' she said.

But, on the contrary, he'd said everything.

Keeping Secrets

1

Detective Inspector Casey Clunes pretended not to notice young PC Walsh as, not quite hidden among the thicket beyond the track where she stood, he reacquainted himself with that day's canteen lunch-time special.

What lay at her feet was just another body. That's what PC Lennon, the assorted team of ambulance personnel and the forensics team must be seeing, too. But the years of service they'd clocked up between them all stood at double figures. Poor Ian Walsh had only been in the force three months. So far, his worst experience of violence on the job was probably witnessing someone's bloody nose, acquired after chucking-out time on a Friday night. Messy, but hardly traumatic. But seeing his undisguised reaction to what each person present had also witnessed reminded her with a dreadful pang just how inured to brutal death her job had made her over the years.

The victim, a middle-aged woman, lay spread-eagled at her feet at the bottom of the rough track that ran through Beecher's Wood. She lay awkwardly, her face covered in dark blood, her skirt riding immodestly over her hefty thighs. This was no accident, Casey was sure of that. A fall from her bike — which lay upended some metres away, its front wheel badly dented — would account for the bruises on her legs and the scratches on her arms, but if she'd simply ridden over a stone or a branch, Casey surmised, she would surely have fallen headlong on her face, not ended up, as she was now, on her back.

So far, the only thing that had been established was that she'd been dead roughly between three and five hours. No murder weapon had yet been found. All Casey could come up with was this: what if she'd been on her way somewhere when someone stepped out in front of her, causing her to brake sharply and lose control of the bike? Once on the ground, dazed and shaken, she'd have been unable to put up much resistance to the frenzied attack that followed.

'So. Who is she?'

It was a casual question. Casey watched as jovial old Dr Philips, the police doctor, snapped one more shot, humming beneath his breath. He could have been taking holiday snaps, she mused.

She'd already gone through the contents of the black mockcroc bag found on the body. A careful cyclist, the victim knew enough about making it difficult for any opportunist to snatch her property not to have kept her bag in her bicycle basket, but to have slung it crosswise over her shoulder instead, from where Casey had, with gloved hands, carefully extricated and bagged the contents. Just a pity the poor woman hadn't taken an equally circumspect approach to her personal safety, she mused.

'Sheila Flynn, according to the cards she carried,' Casey said. 'Mrs, most likely.'

She nodded in the direction of the victim's left hand.

'Somebody certainly had it in for her,' Dr Philips said cheerfully, as he went about his job.

It was Friday. End of the month. Maybe Sheila Flynn had been on her way to deposit some of her wages into her account. What else would explain the bundle of notes in her bag? Two hundred pounds at least at first glance — no doubt earned from a cash-in-hand job since these days most people's earnings went straight into their bank accounts.

'Whoever did this didn't seem to be in it for the money,' Casey said, waving the bundle of notes at Dr Philips.

'What else?'

'Store cards, credit cards, a huge bunch of keys. A building society savings account book containing a pretty tidy amount, too. Not to mention the usual paraphernalia you'd find in a woman's handbag.'

'Any address?'

Casey shook her head. 'I'd guess she's local, though,' she said. 'You'd have to know your way to attempt to cut through this part of Beecher's Wood, particularly at this time of year, when everything's still growing like smoke.'

Fastidiously, she brushed her new linen skirt in an attempt to dislodge something unsavoury she'd picked up from a patch of creeping vegetation.

'Looking for clues among all this — nature — is going to be a nightmare,' she added.

She didn't think it was a bad guess to say that Sheila Flynn probably came this way regularly. Exactly like the poor blighter who found her, she couldn't help thinking. What a dreadful thing to come face-to-face with when you were out walking your dog. Someone would have to go and have a word, check he was OK. Shock could do funny things to people.

She glanced over at PC Walsh. His colour was coming back, thank goodness, and he was even managing to look busy, purposefully swishing a stick around in the undergrowth, presumably looking for clues. A face-saving exercise for sure. Not that she blamed him. Not with Tony Lennon lurking nearby, no doubt already rehearsing his version of events for the lads later, back at the canteen.

It was time to have a word. Sharply, she called Lennon over. There was insolence in that macho strut of his and he had to be made to see that she could do macho, too, if it was called for.

'Found anything yet?' she said coolly.

He flashed her his usual packed-with-pulling-power grin; as usual she ignored it.

'If you ask me, young Walsh has muddied the scene, Inspector,' he said. 'Throwing up his lunch all over the place like that.'

Her eyes held his fearlessly until Lennon's smile diminished to nothing.

'Not a word about Walsh, Lennon,' she said. 'Do you hear me, Officer?'

'Hadn't even crossed my mind, Inspector.'

The reply might have tripped off his tongue, but when he quickly dropped his eyes she knew she'd shaken him.

'Inspector! Over here!'

PC Walsh's cry came from halfway up the woody incline down which Sheila Flynn had cycled earlier. Immediately, they both spun round to see him crouching beside the mottled truck of a gnarled old tree. Evidence, she prayed. And if it was, then thank God it was Walsh who'd found it and not Lennon.

'Stay there,' she called out to him. 'Don't touch anything.'

'Some kind of fibres round the base of this tree,' he said, when Casey had stumbled up the path to join him.

'Not much but it's enough for Forensics to get their teeth into as a start.'

'And now look here, Inspector.'

With one agile movement PC Walsh whipped over to the other side of the path, positioning himself behind another tree — a sturdier, healthier-looking one this time.

'It'd be dead easy to hide yourself behind this tree. Unless someone were looking out for you, you'd get away with it,' he said.

Ian Walsh's puppy-dog enthusiasm made Casey so want him to be right.

'And you think that's what someone did? Rather than step out in front of them, which is what I thought?'

'I do, Inspector. Let's just suppose they

knew her route. All it took was for them to get here first, tie the rope round that tree, pull it across the path to their hiding-place behind this tree, and then, at the right moment, give it a yank.'

Casey stroked her chin as she pictured the scene.

'Then, as she lay sprawled on the ground, dazed and confused, wondering what had happened, back comes the perpetrator and strikes her on the head,' she added. 'Nice work, Constable.'

He pulled himself up to his full height, clearly delighted by her praise.

'I've got an address for the victim, too,' he said, handing her his notebook. 'Checked out the frame reference on the bike and radioed it in.'

She took the notebook from him with a smile.

'I'm impressed, Constable Walsh,' she said.

The bike had been registered to Sheila Flynn of 27 Waverley Way, Brockhaven. Casey made a snap decision to take PC Walsh along to break the news to her next-of-kin. She wanted to see if he was as good with people as he was sharp at spotting evidence. And she still wasn't sure about Lennon. It might be nice to rub his nose in it a bit more by involving Walsh rather than him in the unravelling of this case.

On the journey to Waverley Way — which lay on the edge of town on the recently-built Merryfield Estate — a nervous PC Walsh returned to the subject of what had happened to him at the crime scene.

'Think of it as a rite of passage,' Casey said cheerfully.

At her words his hands relaxed on the wheel.

'You mean you've thrown up, too?'

'Worse,' she admitted. 'Passed out. Take a left here, would you?'

They'd arrived on the outskirts of the sprawling estate, a warren of rabbit-hutch houses and treeless streets, jam-packed with parked cars. Casey thought of her own roomy apartment slap-bang at the end of Brockhaven's main shopping street, with its high ceilings and huge bay windows.

She'd go nuts in no time if she had to live in one of these shoeboxes. Nuttier if she had to share it with a husband and two or three kids — which presumably the majority of the residents of the Merryfield Estate did.

PC Walsh's words broke into her thoughts.

'It must be difficult, though, not letting work intrude on your personal life,' he said.

'Let's just say I don't let it spoil my mealtimes,' she said. 'I let the canteen food do that.'

PC Walsh's hearty chuckle was so endearing that she was almost tempted to take him into her confidence. How would he react, she wondered, if she were to tell him that right now her personal life was at a very low ebb and that the bigger the eruption of crime in Brockhaven the better.

The busier she was kept solving it, the easier it would be to avoid Dom. She tried to ignore the tiny voice in her head. 'Stop closing your ears,' it said. 'Confront him,' it said. 'March into his office and do that 'we need to talk' thing they do so well on the soaps but that nobody ever really does in real life,' it said.

'Then ask him straight. Was it a joke, all that stuff about feeling stifled here in Brockhaven? All that complaining about the most exciting story you'd had recently being the one about insider dealing among the parish council? Which turned out to be no more controversial than co-opting the vicar's wife on to the harvest festival committee without the chair's knowledge.'

She knew there were other questions, too. Like, exactly how serious Dom was about leaving the *Gazette*. And had he thought what it might mean to their relationship if he went off to London to work on one of the dailies and she stayed here?

How she hated all this personal stuff! 'Yeah,' the little voice nagged. 'That's why you choose to ignore it in the hope that it will go away. Hiding behind your work, that's all you're doing. Coward!'

Gritting her teeth, Casey put her foot on the brake, silencing the nagging once and for all. She was here to do a job and Dom Talbot would just have to stand in line.

'This is it, PC Walsh. Another first for you, I'm guessing. Draw up at the next house, please. Oh, and straighten your tie, would you?'

They'd already agreed beforehand that PC Walsh was to be the one to break the dreadful news. He wanted to do it, he said, and Casey didn't try to talk him out of it.

It was a man in his fifties who opened the door. Middling height and weight was her first impression, before her eyes hit his stomach, which strained the buttons of his blue and white check shirt. His complexion told a tale of fast food and lack of fresh air. Casey wondered if he might have a heart condition and worried about the effect the news he was about to hear might have on him.

His gaze wandered from PC Walsh to her then back to PC Walsh again. She recognised the panic in the man's eyes. He knew, she decided. Of course he knew. His next words confirmed it.

'Sheila!' he said. 'Tell me it's not Sheila.'

'Mr Flynn, can we come inside?' PC Walsh said.

'Get him inside and sitting down before you say a word,' she'd hissed at him just as they were getting out of the car. 'And then just tell him. No beating about the bush.'

'You're right, of course, Inspector,' he'd said. 'Let's just get on with it, shall we?'

In the end, he acquitted himself quite well, addressing Mr Flynn gently but firmly. The body of a woman had been found badly beaten about the head just after two o'clock this afternoon, at the bottom of the path that ran as a short cut through Beecher's Wood. Of course, PC Walsh refrained from saying just how badly she'd been beaten. By the time it came round to the moment Sheila Flynn's husband would be forced to identify her, they'd have cleaned her up.

'I knew there was something, but I never expected this.' Mr Flynn sank his head in his hands. Then he added, 'She said she'd be here for lunch. I'd come home from school especially to see her.'

From his clothes and his strong local accent, Casey didn't have him down as a teacher, and he had workman's hands. His forehead glistened with a film of sweat and his complexion had gone from pasty to grey. Swiftly, Casey rose and found her way to the kitchen. A glass of water was required if she wasn't much mistaken. When she returned, Mr Flynn had his head between his knees.

'Is there anyone we can call, Mr Flynn?' PC Walsh was saying. 'A neighbour? A relative, perhaps?'

'My son'll be back soon,' the man muttered. 'Kevin.'

'Can we ring him, sir? If he's at work we can easily send a car.'

Mr Flynn was sitting up now, sipping at the water.

'Work? Our Kevin? I don't think so. Down the pub, most likely.'

Leaning forward, he placed the glass shakily on the highly polished glass coffee table. It looked new, Casey mused. Expensive, and very this season. Her mind dwelled for a moment on the

158

bundle of notes she'd found in Sheila Flynn's handbag.

PC Walsh cleared his throat nervously. 'Well, does he have a phone, sir? I really don't think you should be alone just now.'

'He should be here,' the man grumbled. 'He said he'd run Sheila out to the garden centre to pick up some garden furniture in the sale when she got back from work. I just nipped home for half an hour to check he'd kept his word. Which he hasn't, of course. Just let 'em deliver it, Sheila, if you know what you want, he said. Money no object. They charge fifteen quid to deliver. Can you believe it? Flamin' liberty.'

PC Walsh glanced uneasily at Casey. There was panic in his eyes. She understood exactly what was going on in his head; he would have expected hysterical grief or stunned disbelieving silence from the victim's widower. He couldn't possibly have primed himself for this discomfiting display of garrulousness.

'Mr Flynn,' Casey said gently. 'What do you know about your wife's movements today?'

Tomorrow or the next day they would have to return and question him about his own movements, callous as that might sound, but for now she had a script to follow.

'Where was she going this morning, Mr Flynn? Can you tell us?'

The man looked from one to the other of them, clearly bewildered. Casey would have bet that Sheila Flynn, like most wives, would have told her husband exactly where she was going this morning, and probably every morning. Whether her husband retained the information or not would have been a different matter.

'Sheila has a lot of different jobs,' he said vaguely.

'What sort of jobs, Mr Flynn?'

'Cleaning, babysitting, that type of thing.'

She'd been right, then. Cash-in-hand jobs. The image of the wad of notes she'd seen in Sheila Flynn's handbag flashed up in front of her.

'Wait a minute,' Mr Flynn said. Something suddenly seemed to occur to him. 'It's Friday today. She does the Shaws on Fridays, I'm pretty sure. Yeah, that's right.

Monday, Wednesday and Friday mornings it's the Shaws. Tuesdays it's the Endecotts.'

'Endecotts Electronics?' PC Walsh butted in.

'That's right,' Mr Flynn replied. 'Big house. Rolling in it. Workaholics, my Sheila says. Teenage daughter. Never sees her mum and dad.'

From giving the initial impression that he had little firm knowledge of his wife's daily routine, Mr Flynn had suddenly veered in the opposite direction. He'd be telling them the colour of the Endecotts' bath towels next, Casey mused. It was time to get him back on track.

'Have you got an address for the Shaws, Mr Flynn?'

He looked at her as dumbfounded as if she'd asked him to recite the *Lord's Prayer* in Latin. It was no matter. She knew Shaws. The estate agents' premises were on the High Street. She'd even been inside once or twice back in her flat-hunting days. Most of the property on offer was either out of her league financially or for short-term let. As for the address of the family home, PC Walsh was already on his mobile, ringing through to check it out.

'Forresters Drive,' he said, after a minute. 'Number 12. 'The Glades'.'

'Aye, that sounds like it,' Mr Flynn interjected. 'Posh side. Out by the golf course.'

Casey and PC Walsh exchanged glances. That squared with where Sheila Flynn had been found, at least.

'She left about eight-thirty,' he said. 'It takes her a good thirty minutes to cycle.'

Only this morning she hadn't arrived. She would have been almost at the end of her journey through the wood when the killer struck.

It was a fair ride, he was saying now, but it had always been worth Sheila's while, because not only was he — the husband, presumably, so Casey decided — the estate agent who looked after the letting of a group of holiday cottages, which always meant more work for Sheila if she wanted it, but there was also quite a bit of babysitting in it for her, too.

PC Walsh's pen flew across the page in a reckless dash to keep up with Mr

Flynn's chaotic monologue.

'Though, strictly speaking, the son's not a baby,' he added. 'Unless you count what's going on his head, which, according to Sheila, is nothing very much. They've had the ground floor made over for him — no expense spared — because he's stuck in a wheelchair and he's far too big nowadays for Mrs Shaw to lift him. That's where Sheila sometimes comes — came — in useful.'

The change in tense wasn't lost on Casey. Making the transition from present to past tense was a sure sign that, finally, the truth had hit home. His wife was never coming back. Casey handed Mr Flynn the glass of water, which so far he'd barely touched. This time he took it gratefully, swiftly emptying the contents.

Casey's thoughts returned to Sheila Flynn. She'd taken note of the victim's sturdy legs. Her flimsy jacket had presumably hidden a pair of equally sturdy arms and shoulders. Had she made any attempt to fight back at her attacker? If so there'd be some evidence of skin tissue, fibres, hair maybe. Maybe

163

Forensics were already on to something.

Who could be responsible for this crime? She was even surer now that the culprit was a local man. You'd have to know that short cut as well as Sheila Flynn had — as well as the man with the dog who'd found her had. Before they'd left the crime scene for the Flynns' house, Casey had despatched Lennon — who had taken his orders with badly-concealed ill grace — to the man's house. There was probably nothing to be suspicious of about the man's story, but many an investigation had been led up the garden path because a trivial enquiry had been left unmade.

There was the sound of a key turning in the lock. All eyes turned towards the door.

'Kevin. He must have run out of money. Or friends,' Mr Flynn added scornfully.

The front door led straight into the living room. Kevin Flynn, his hand wrestling with the key in the lock, regarded the group of three with an expression that was hard to read.

Like his father, he was dressed in jeans,

trainers and a blue checked shirt, with the sleeves rolled up above his elbows, only on his lean frame everything was a much better fit. Like his father, he had a pasty complexion, acquired no doubt from sharing the same diet. He was a couple of years off thirty, she surmised, but if he kept up the pub lifestyle Mr Flynn had hinted at, his flat stomach would pretty soon be turning into a paunch to compare with his father's.

Kevin Flynn glared at his father as if he suspected him personally responsible for calling in the police. It flashed through Casey's mind that he may have a guilty conscience. Where did he get his money from to spend his days in the pub if he didn't work?

'What's all this, then?'

'I'm afraid we have some news, Mr Flynn,' PC Walsh said, as smoothly as if he'd been doing this all his life.

'Oh yeah?'

Kevin Flynn eyed PC Walsh suspiciously. He was still at the door, his hand on the key, as if he couldn't quite make his mind up whether to come in or not.

'It's your mother, Mr Flynn. I'm afraid she's dead.'

Casey would have laid odds that Kevin Flynn was the type of man to keep his emotions to himself. So when he fell to his knees with a strangled yelp of pain, dropping the house key as he flung his arms around himself as if for protection, she was completely taken aback.

'Mum. Mum. Oh, Mum,' he moaned over and over, clutching now at his head and pawing at the floor like a maltreated dog.

Simultaneously, she and PC Walsh made a move towards him, but were stopped in their tracks by Mr Flynn's next words.

'No, Kevin. It's not your mum that's dead. Get up!' he shouted. 'Your mum's fine, as far as I know. It's Sheila that's dead. She's been found murdered in Beecher's Wood.'

Casey was gripped by a disturbing feeling of embarrassment and a quick glance at PC Walsh confirmed her suspicion that he shared it. They'd both made a stupid assumption about Sheila

Flynn's relationship to Kevin Flynn. Clearly Sheila Flynn was Kevin's stepmother, not his real mother. They'd delivered a mistaken-identity faux pas worthy of a re-run on a sitcom. If it wasn't so tragic it would have been hilarious!

Kevin stumbled to his feet, brushing the dust away from his jeans foolishly. When he finally spoke, it was in disbelief.

'What do you mean, murdered? She can't be. She's at work,' he said.

Suddenly, he seemed to remember something. 'Oh, God. I forgot,' he groaned, putting his hand to his head and running it through his oily hair. 'She rang. You'd gone to work, Dad. I didn't think it was anything to worry you about so I left it.'

'Sheila rang here?' Casey said sharply. 'What time? What did she say? Was she in any danger?'

There'd been no trace of a mobile phone. Maybe the murderer had lunged towards her and kicked it out of her hands as she'd desperately tried to make a call for help, and it was still there somewhere, hidden among the trees.

Maybe he'd picked it up and it was on his person. In that case, if they had the number they'd easily be able to put a trace on it and the case would be solved in no time.

Kevin Flynn flicked his tongue over his lips.

'No. Not Sheila, She never rang. It was that woman. That one with the kid.' he said. 'She left a message.'

No quick solution, then. Casey might have known this wasn't going to be so simple. 'A couple of messages, maybe,' he added sullenly.

Kevin Flynn obviously worked on a need-to-know basis, Casey decided. Her initial impressions of him as being shifty hadn't changed. On the contrary, she was even surer that here was a man who spent his life covering his tracks.

'When, Mr Flynn? Did you erase it? Is it still on the phone?' Casey moved swiftly to the phone and tapped in 1571. 'I heard it ringing but I just went back to sleep,' Kevin Flynn said, his expression hang-dog.

Casey leaned back on her heels to listen

to the messages. The first one was restrained, but with an edge that suggested that the speaker was struggling to maintain politeness.

'Sheila? It's Helen Shaw here. It's ten past nine. I'm sure you've left and you'll probably turn up outside my house any minute now, so this phone call's probably a waste of time.'

The second call had been made twenty minutes later. This time the voice was sharp and the words were clipped.

'I don't know where you are, Sheila, but wherever it is, it's not here. I hoped after our little chat the other week that you understood just how important an issue timekeeping was for me. Clearly I was wrong. I'm sorry you think so little of me — and of Jack — that you haven't even bothered to ring up and explain just why you aren't coming in this morning.'

At this point she broke off briefly. Casey wondered if she might be reassuring someone — Jack, her son? — that she wouldn't be long. When she resumed, the pitch of her voice had gone up a notch. Here was someone who'd lost it big time.

'Don't bother coming in next Monday, Sheila,' she yelled. 'Or any other day, come to that. I'll be advertising for someone reliable to help me out. You've failed to turn up once too often and, quite frankly, both Drew and I could kill you right now!'

Nice choice of words, Casey mused, as she pressed the button to save the message and replaced the receiver.

2

The usual early Saturday morning sounds woke Casey from a troubled sleep. In the garden of the Lord Nelson, which backed on to her flat, last night's wine bottles — empty now, of course — cascaded into the recycling bins in a deafening crescendo. The High Street was already clogged with slow-moving cars, all scavenging for the prime parking spots. It was another sunny day in Brockhaven, in an Indian summer that showed no signs of coming to an end.

Casey threw open the bread bin to check if the bread fairy had visited in the night. (She hadn't, of course.) Dry weather was something to be cheerful about anyway. It meant that the chances of finding some more clues in the vicinity of Beecher's Wood were still good.

She helped herself to the dregs of the box of muesli, which was all she had in her cupboard of a breakfasty nature. She only had herself to blame if the contents of her bowl resembled sawdust — no amount of nagging from Dom had managed to cure her of her habit of creaming off the box's entire ration of fruit and nuts in one fell swoop, so that after the first helping there was precious little of anything tasty left.

'But it's my heap of sawdust,' Casey reminded herself. 'And as long as I live on my own I can do as I please.' Up until that walk down the pier last week, she would have felt smug at this realisation.

But right now she didn't feel smug at all. There was an intruder trying to get into her head and that intruder was Dom Talbot. Casey laid down her bowl of mush. Nine months they had been dating. Back then she'd been in pokey digs and hated it. Dom had lived — and still did — a couple of miles outside Brockhaven in the tiny cottage he'd inherited from his granny.

Maybe it was envy that had sent her on a quest for her own place to live. Whatever the reason, it had made her feel — at the age of twenty-nine — properly grown up at last. She'd revelled in the space and in small ways had celebrated her independence daily, counting her blessings each time she looked up at her high ceiling or out through the bay windows that let in so much light.

Her mother — had she been alive — would have said she had it all. Career, car, flat — a perfect trio of achievement. The icing on the cake was Dom, who made her roar with laughter and her body sing, who'd opened her eyes to books and poetry — stuff she'd never properly enjoyed at school — and who seemed to like her just as much as she liked him. She'd thought she and Dom were solid. But maybe she'd been wrong.

They'd been taking a walk down the pier. Where they met at the horizon in a blue haze, sky and sea were indistinguishable and the sea breeze was so light it barely lifted your hair. Dom was quiet. She should have felt suspicious because normally he could have decimated the leg count in a donkey sanctuary. But the heat and the sun had put her in a walking trance, emptying her mind of everything but the pleasure of being alive on such a glorious day.

In fact, it had been Casey herself who'd broken the silence.

'I never thought I'd say this, being a city girl,' she'd said, scrunching her eyes against the glare of the hot sun. 'But I don't think there's anywhere more perfect than the English seaside on a day like this.'

When Dom had grunted by way of reply, Casey had assumed it was in agreement. But then he'd said, 'Don't you miss it, though? London? The buzz, being at the centre of everything? I wish I worked on one of the big dailies,' he'd added with a sigh.

Just then, with Dom's words still hanging in the air, a small child perilously in charge of an ice-cream came flying towards them from the opposite direction. When he tripped and lost his footing, the ensuing mayhem came as a huge relief to Casey. Dom had livened up after that and Casey had decided to let the subject lie.

Why couldn't things stay the same? She

wasn't ready to hear that Dom was thinking of making changes in his life, however tenuous. In fact, all week she'd been deleting his messages and switching him to answerphone. Let him think she was swamped with work.

Fact was, she was scared. If Dom had had enough of the *Brockhaven Gazette* then maybe it meant he had had enough of her.

Her phone suddenly sprang into life. Reaching for it, Casey read Dom's name. She let it ring. If he was dumping her, then he was going to have to tell her to her face.

* * *

PCs Walsh and Lennon had been wandering their beat for a couple of hours in tense silence. PC Lennon had decided he wasn't really speaking to Walshy after yesterday, when he'd had his wrists slapped by Detective Inspector Clunes. PC Walsh had been made physically ill by the sight of Sheila Flynn's injuries, to the mocking scorn of PC Lennon. Ian Walsh, not having been privy to Lennon's dressing down, had so far been unable to work out what he'd done to offend his partner. In the end he put it down to the heat and the extra ten pounds Tony carried. It was a relief when his radio crackled into life.

They drew to a standstill and listened as the details came out. Young girl caught shoplifting at La Ropa — dress shop on the High Street.

'That's handy,' PC Walsh said. 'It's only across the road. How lucky is that!'

PC Lennon glared at him.

'Not very, considering we're due to go off on our break in about thirty minutes. Now we'll be lucky to get a sit-down for another two hours.'

PC Walsh decided that he preferred the silence.

The shop was small and very, very pricey. Once inside, the two officers wrestled their way past rails of women's clothes into the minute space that contained just one changing room and the till area.

The owner was leaning up against the

counter. Even though she was clearly harassed, PC Walsh thought she was very attractive for an older woman, and from the way Lennon was staring at her it was clear he wasn't the only one to think so.

The alleged shoplifter sat perched on the edge of a chair next to the till. Jiggling first one foot and then the other, she sat on her hands, scowling.

'Jail bait,' PC Lennon thought, taking in the make-up and the tiny skirt. 'Fifteen if she's a day.' Why were they even bothering to arrest her?

'She thought she could just walk in here and take my property,' the owner said in heavily accented English.

'Don't point, it's rude,' the girl growled.

The shop owner glared back.

'You watch your mouth, young lady,' PC Lennon retorted. 'You're in enough trouble as it is.'

'Whatever,' the girl muttered.

The shop owner raised her eyes heavenwards. Her expression suggested that only in England did teenage girls speak to their elders and betters with such disrespect.

'There was no one in the shop but me and her,' she said. 'I went out the back to get a bottle of water. I didn't think it was a risk if I kept the curtain open.'

She cast her eyes in the direction of a pink satin curtain that divided the front of the shop from the private quarters.

'I couldn't believe it! She took two tops from the rail and slipped them into her bag. Quite brazenly!'

To prove it, she grabbed the copious yellow and blue straw basket sitting at the girl's feet, drew the items out and waved them in front of the officers' eyes.

'One hundred and forty pounds each,' she said.

If PC Walsh was meant to be impressed, he wasn't much. He spent as little as possible on clothes.

'Have you got anything to say, young lady?' PC Lennon said.

The girl shook her head sullenly.

'You don't deny it?' PC Walsh thought it only right to give her a second chance. All that 'young lady' stuff would put anyone's back up.

She sighed and finally looked at him

with clear blue eyes. No sign of drugs, then, he mused. 'Look, officer,' she said, holding out her wrists. 'Can we just get on with it? My name is Alicia Endecott and I live at 1 Fairway View. Now, are you going to put the cuffs on?'

* * *

Back at the station, Casey checked her 'to do' list. Now that Kevin Flynn had identified the body — Mr Flynn had been far too upset to do it himself — it was OK to release the name of the victim to the Press.

Since the Press in Brockhaven usually meant Dom Talbot, she decided to get someone else on to that. She felt no more inclined to speak to him now than she had earlier. In the end she'd deleted the message he'd left even before listening to it.

Drawing a line through 'identification', she went on to the next item on her list. *Visit Helen Shaw*. One more thing she could cross off. Her visit to the Shaws this morning had shown her that however threatening the poor woman had sounded in the message she'd left for Sheila Flynn, the idea of her murdering anyone was simply fanciful.

She'd been alone with her son, which had rather taken Casey by surprise; it being Saturday she'd expected Mr Shaw would be there, too. The boy — he'd be about eleven or twelve, Casey imagined — was clearly severely disabled.

He sat in a wheelchair, a plaid rug pulled over his knees even though the hot summer sun streamed through the French windows. His head rolled back continuously and his luminously white stick-thin arms thrashed the air in unco-ordinated movements. Occasionally a shrill animal cry escaped him.

He didn't seem to have noticed Casey walk into the room, and even when his mother spoke to him she saw no sign of recognition in his eyes. But Helen Shaw's look of devotion, as she carefully wiped his hands and face with a damp cloth, was unmistakable.

'Don't feel sorry for me, Inspector,' Mrs Shaw said curtly. 'I know it must be difficult for you to imagine why I choose to keep Jack here at home with me instead of putting him into residential care. But he's my son and I love him. He belongs here with his family.'

The words sounded like a practised script she'd delivered many times. Casey felt ashamed because that was exactly what she'd been thinking. How many faces must Helen Shaw have looked into and seen the same embarrassment and non-comprehension that she herself must be exhibiting now?

'It must be difficult for you on your own,' she'd said.

Mrs Shaw shrugged. Her wild hair framed her face and the ill-matching skirt and top she wore were evidence of this woman's total lack of 'me' time. No wonder she was furious when she thought Sheila Flynn had let her down.

'My husband's understaffed,' she'd replied. 'It's a very busy time of year for estate agents and poor Drew's been working twenty-four seven recently.'

Not only a devoted mother, but a devoted wife, too. While she spoke she cleared the breakfast things away into the dishwasher. It was as if she were on autopilot, Casey mused. How many times a day did she repeat these same chores, and for what love in return? As soon as this thought occurred to her she felt ashamed. Not everybody's as selfish as you, Clunes, she told herself.

'What's this about, anyway, Inspector?'

When Casey told her the news of Sheila Flynn's death, Helen Shaw had covered her face with her hands and sat down heavily on to a chair.

'Tell me about your relationship with Mrs Flynn,' Casey said, when she'd given her enough time to compose herself.

'She was my cleaner. She helped me with Jack. Oh my God!' Lifting her head from her hands and looking horrified, she added, 'I phoned her yesterday. I said I wished she was dead!'

'I'm not here to arrest you, Mrs Shaw,' Casey said. 'We all say things like that when we're under stress. And from what I understand you'd grown used to her letting you down.'

'You listened to my call, then? Of

course you did,' she said, answering her own question. 'At first I thought she was a godsend. Nothing was too much trouble. But just recently . . . I know Jack's not easy, but suddenly, as well as her time-keeping getting bad, it was as if she resented everything I asked her to do.'

'When did this change begin?'

'I can't really remember, but it was almost an overnight thing. One day she was ordering me to go and put my feet up and the next she was making her excuses and leaving half an hour earlier than we'd agreed.' Cautiously, she added, 'And there was something else.'

Casey steeled herself. 'Go on,' she said.

'Drew said I was imagining it, but I swear I wasn't,' she said. 'It was the way she looked at me. As if she despised me. I couldn't understand the change in her — it wasn't as if I didn't pay her well for her trouble.'

'So by yesterday you'd already decided pretty much to let her go?' Very interesting indeed, Casey thought.

Helen nodded. 'It was the last straw — her not turning up like that. Of course, had I known . . . '

She tailed off as Jack took up a loud wailing.

'If you'll excuse me, Inspector. Toilet visit.'

At that point Casey had excused herself pretty quickly. Now she sat at her desk musing over what she'd said. What had changed Sheila Flynn from a woman for whom nothing was too much trouble into the lazy, uncaring person with sloppy time-keeping that Helen Shaw had described?

'I'm not going to have them in on my interview! I can speak for myself!'

From somewhere in the station those words, shrieked at high volume, assaulted her ears. Who on earth was that interrupting her train of thought? She shot up from her seat.

At the desk, Alicia Endecott was doing her utmost to disarm herself from PC Lennon's grip. PC Walsh, arms folded, looked on, clearly enjoying the spectacle of Lennon practically wrestled to the floor by a girl half his size. Mr and Mrs Endecott stood by like two nervous, hopping cats, trying to reason with their daughter. Casey got the distinct impression that they were wishing they could be anywhere but here.

'It's the law, Alicia, darling! You're a minor. You have to have an adult present.'

Mrs Endecott's tone was wheedling — the voice of a woman afraid to discipline her child.

'In that case, get me another adult!'

Alicia Endecott had finally stopped beating up PC Lennon. Summoning all his dignity as he righted his cap, he addressed Casey.

'We could always get Social Services, ma'am,' he said.

Forty minutes later, the tape running, Casey began her interview with Alicia Endecott. Also present were PC Walsh, and a female social worker whose expression said she wasn't best pleased at losing her Saturday afternoon for this stroppy little madam.

Casey surveyed the fifteen-year-old girl sulking in her chair. There was a great deal of make-up. She'd also been over-generous with the hair product. On her pale, plump feet she wore a snazzy pair of orange sequinned slippers, of the kind you could pick up for a song — the ones stitched by exploited Chinese children, Casey decided. She probably had a pair in every colour available.

'So tell me, Alicia. What makes a girl like you, with all your advantages, feel the need to take to shoplifting?' Casey leaned forward in her chair.

Alicia declined to answer. Instead she turned her attentions to her nails, picking off the lurid mauve polish in flakes. They drifted to the floor like petals.

'Is it for the buzz? Or was it a dare?'

Again no answer.

'Come on, Alicia. Give me a break. You can't need the things you stole. For one thing they were both size eight.' Alicia looked a healthy twelve.

'I took them to sell,' she said, finally breaking her vow of silence. 'At school.'

The social worker gave Casey a look that said, 'I could have told you that.' The phrase 'peer pressure' ran through Casey's head. Poor little rich girl, out of her depth at Brockhaven High. How could she shed her pony-club image and get in with the in crowd? Yeah — nicking designer gear and flogging in it in the playground would have done it.

'It's not what you think.' Her next words came out in a rush. 'I've got this — boyfriend. Warren. I love him.'

'Did he persuade you to do this, Alicia?' PC Walsh said.

'No! Warren had nothing to do with it!' She was irate now. 'It was her! That Mrs Flynn. My mum's cleaner! She made me do it!'

Casey's blood froze.

Mumbling into her fingers, now fully stripped of polish, Alicia added, 'She said she was going to tell my mum and dad.'

'Tell them what, Alicia?'

'We'd skived off school. We were in bed together. How was I to know it was the cleaner's day to come in?' Alicia Endecott suddenly looked about twelve as she crumpled into tears.

Casey sat forward in her chair. The investigation had suddenly taken a dramatically different turn.

'Are you saying she was blackmailing you?'

Alicia nodded.

'For the tape, please, Alicia,' PC Walsh said.

'Yes!' She glared at him. 'I had no choice! My parents hated Warren. They said he wasn't good enough for me. Just because he lives on the Merryfield Estate. I had to get her off my back.'

From her tone it was hard to say who she felt most contempt for — her parents or their cleaning lady!

'How many times have you stolen things, Alicia?'

The girl's eyes flickered as she gave her answer. 'Only this once.'

Casey didn't believe her, but she didn't think a visit to the playground at Brockhaven High would furnish her with the truth.

'Warren didn't know I'd done it.' she insisted again. 'He said we should ignore her. She was just a daft old cow. He said it'd be better if I got her sacked.'

Nice type, Casey mused. Maybe Mr and Mrs Endecott weren't such bad judges of character after all.

'Do you love Warren, Alicia?'

'He stopped the other girls bullying me. Nobody dares do anything now I'm Warren's girlfriend. He's in year Eleven.' She looked proudly at Casey.

'And you, Alicia? What year are you in?'

'Year Nine.'

When she caught PC Walsh's eye, she was careful to keep her face impassive.

'What happens now?' Alicia spoke through a mouth full of bunched up fingers.

'You'll be summoned to appear before the magistrate in due course,' Casey said. 'Meanwhile, I think I should ring your parents and tell them to come and collect you.'

Alicia jumped up from her seat. Her voice was frantic.

'No! They'll kill me. They don't know about — what Warren and me . . . '

Casey thought hard. She'd like to have a word with this Warren. If Sheila Flynn had been in the business of digging for dirt in order to supplement her wages, she wouldn't have had to dig far to get something on Warren. It looked like it had been handed to her on a plate.

'What if you rang Warren and told him where you are?' Casey suggested. 'Do you think he might come and collect you? If he loves you — like you say he does — then surely he won't want to leave you to face the music on your own?'

Alicia relaxed at last. 'Yeah. Great idea. Thanks,' she said, almost — though not quite — showing gratitude.

* * *

'Nice-looking boy, Alicia,' Casey whispered, as she and Alicia waited at the desk, some thirty minutes later, for the young man in question to amble across the yard and into the building.

Alicia simpered. Clearly she was besotted. She feasted her eyes on him as he strode towards her and took her in his embrace. Casey was touched in spite of herself. It wasn't hard to see the attraction on her side. But what did he see in her? she wondered. She was pretty enough but surely Warren Smith, with his status, could have had his pick?

'What yer bin doin', yer daft gel?'

'I had to tell them about Mrs Flynn, Warren. It's the truth, isn't it, so they're going to have to arrest her and she'll get in much more trouble than I will.'

If Alicia Endecott hadn't heard about Sheila's fate — and Casey hadn't seen it as having any relevance in their recent interview — it soon became apparent her boyfriend was much better informed. Even as Alicia spat out her words, his expression changed from solicitude to sheer horror.

'She's dead, Alicia! It's been on the local news all morning!'

'What!' She spun round to face Casey. 'Is this right?'

Casey nodded.

'Gone and got herself murdered. You've got yourself in trouble for nothing.' Warren looked to Casey for support.

The milk of human kindness was clearly severely rationed with this young man, she decided. That didn't make him a murderer, of course. Although if he was being blackmailed for the crime she was about to accuse him of it did suggest he had a motive.

Stepping forward, her hand on his arm, Casey cleared her throat.

'Warren Smith, I'm arresting you under the Sexual Offences Act,' she said and proceeded to caution him.

'What you talkin' about? I ain't done nuffin'.'

'How old are you, Warren?'

'Two months off of seventeen,' he said.

'In that case, we'll have to see what the courts have to say about your activities with a minor.'

3

Drew knew he was taking a risk. He'd promised Helen he would be home by two-thirty to give her a break from Jack. God knows, if anybody needed a break, she did.

That reminded him — first thing Monday he'd advertise for some part-time help.

Sheila Flynn's face rose up in his mind — those narrow cheeks, those cold, indifferent eyes. He'd tried to sound sorry when Helen rang him to tell him all about her visit from that police-woman. She'd sounded shocked and distraught — one more reason why he should be pointing the car in the direction of home.

But even though he'd mouthed the right platitudes, he had only felt elation. Which was why he now found himself driving in the opposite direction from home instead, out towards Blakenthorpe on the coast road — heading for Dove Cottage and Catherine. He had to see her; a week was far too long to be apart. He wanted to lift her up in his arms and bury his face in her sweet-smelling hair. He wanted to tell her that at last they were free of the person who'd been making their lives a misery all this time. And he wanted to tell her that finally he'd decided to leave Helen and — if she would have him — join his life with hers.

She wasn't expecting him. Probably he should call her to tell her he was on his way. But like this he'd catch her unawares, the way he loved to. Maybe she'd be relaxing in a deck-chair under the big old cherry tree, immersed in one of those six-hundred-page historical romances she revelled in. Or, if the heat had driven her indoors, perhaps he'd find her lying on her bed, dozing or simply staring into space.

On occasions when he found her so, he liked to imagine she was thinking of him. But no matter with what speed she donned that sparkling light-hearted mask of hers she was never quick enough to fool Drew. He had grown adept at spotting the chinks through which her grief still revealed itself.

Was he destined to fall in love with women who loved their children — dead or alive — more than they loved him? Catherine's son, Luke, had been put into a coma as a result of a terrible car crash, and now was dead. Then there was Helen, whose love for their son Jack had, over the years, squeezed out any love remaining for himself, however much she denied it.

At the thought of Helen, guilt hovered like a butterfly on the warm air. He brushed it aside, refused to let it settle. Instead he turned up the music as the car licked up the miles and turned his thoughts back to Catherine.

★ ★ ★

Back at the station, in the interview room, sat Warren Smith, cut-off jeans showing his tanned legs to perfection. He eyed Casey nervously.

'So — am I gonna get done for — you know?'

He peered at Casey through a lock of honey-blond hair, his foot tapping the floor repeatedly, betraying his nerves. What was it about teenage girls, she wondered, that attracted them to Warren's type? OK, he might have the attitude but there certainly wasn't much going on upstairs.

The thing to do now was to lead him up the garden path. The chances of a sixteen-year-old being prosecuted for having consensual sex with a fifteen-year-old girl were remote. If he thought she was only interested in this one offence then he might relax his guard when she steered the subject round to Sheila Flynn.

She knew it was wrong to think ill of the dead, but that woman had been a nasty piece of work. There was absolutely no way she would stop at blackmailing Alicia once she got wind of their little secret. She would have had a field day with the likes of Warren Smith!

'Your girlfriend tells me you knew

nothing about Sheila Flynn blackmailing her, Warren,' she said, deliberately choosing to ignore his earlier question. 'Now you can call me an old cynic if you like, but I'm not sure I go along with that.'

His gaze flickered almost imperceptibly. 'I didn't know,' he said, his voice veering away from his carefully cultivated growl and heading for a nervous whine. 'Not for a while, anyway.'

'Tell me, how long have you been seeing Alicia Endecott, Warren?'

His shoulders relaxed. Why, she wondered, did he suddenly give the impression that he felt on safer ground? Because it got them off the subject of Sheila Flynn? In that case, maybe he wasn't as dim as she had first thought. Admitting you'd had under-age sex with your girlfriend was peanuts compared to murdering your girlfriend's cleaner because she was blackmailing you, for instance.

'When you say seeing, do you mean — you know?'

She didn't mean 'you know'. She was hoping for some little insight about why the likes of Warren Smith would go for someone like Alicia Endecott. But if he wanted to think that, let him.

'She's a bit posh for you, wouldn't you say, Warren?'

'No, not really,' he mumbled. 'Not when you get past the accent. Her parents, though . . . '

He raised his eyes heavenwards, like that was all the explanation needed as far the Endecotts were concerned.

'Who started it with you two? Was it you or her?'

'Definitely her. She — '

'So when did you find out Mrs Flynn was blackmailing Alicia, Warren?' she said, stopping him mid-sentence. 'And when did she start blackmailing you?'

* * *

For months they'd been so careful. Brockhaven was a small place. Everyone knew everyone else. Not for them a cosy drink in one of the many pubs, or a stroll along the pier on a sunny afternoon arm in arm. The illicit nature of their relationship had forced them to seek out other places where they could mingle with the crowds unnoticed.

Had it been up to Drew, he would never have left the house. He loved it for its order — such a contrast to the chaos of his own home, centred round Jack's vociferous needs as it was.

But it wasn't good for Catherine to stay inside too long. She grew morose, withdrawing into herself. Even though Luke had been dead a good nine months, coming to terms with his death was no easier for her now than on the day she'd switched off his life-support machine and held his hand, until he slipped away.

That was the day he'd found her wandering the hospital grounds. He was there with Helen and Jack, who was undergoing another of those innumerable checkups that left them both none the wiser but infinitely more exhausted and quarrelsome from all the effort of just getting him there.

Helen had sent him out of the room because his pacing up and down was getting on her nerves. He'd fled in relief and that was when he discovered

Catherine, alone and weeping.

It wasn't the first time he had seen her. Whenever he accompanied Helen — and he always did no matter how often she insisted she could manage on her own — the waiting around gave him plenty of time to observe fellow visitors.

What was her story, he wondered, as his glance fell on yet one more person who, like Helen and himself, was here to wait, and watch and worry.

On that day, he thought Catherine had been beautiful in her pain. He had approached her, gently turning her round and leading her back inside, buying her a coffee and listening while she told him Luke's story.

Helen hadn't missed him when he finally got back. If Catherine and himself were to embark on an affair, she wouldn't even notice. It was a bitter observation but it was to their advantage. Until the day Sheila Flynn, out shopping for the day in Lowestoft, miles away from Brockhaven, spotted them walking hand-in-hand down the main shopping street.

★ ★ ★

'Maybe,' Warren said, 'maybe I wasn't telling you everything when I said I didn't know about Sheila Flynn.'

'Go on, Warren,' Casey replied. 'I'm listening.'

'It was me she started on first. Not Alicia at all, whatever she says.'

At last they were getting somewhere.

'She caught me one day. I thought she'd decided it weren't none of her business — what me and Alicia got up to. Well, it weren't, was it? I'd put it right out my mind. Alicia, though — she was a nervous wreck about it. She kept waiting and worrying for her to say something to her mum and dad.'

'What do you mean, she caught you, Warren?'

He shifted in his seat, avoiding her eyes as he answered.

'It was only a couple of chocolate bars,' he confessed. 'My mum hadn't given me any money for my lunch. Only she saw me slip 'em into my pocket. She said something about how breaking the law seemed to be a bit of a habit with me and what was to stop her going inside and telling the geezer what run the shop.'

He inspected the sole of his trainer, then added, 'I would have shopped myself right there and then if I'd known where that woman was going.'

The direction Sheila Flynn had been going, so Warren told Casey, was a devious one. She wanted money. Fifty pounds a week from each of them would stop her from telling Mr and Mrs Endecott exactly what their precious daughter and her low-life boyfriend were up to when they were out at work every hour God sent making more money in a week than she could make in a year.

'Alicia was dead scared,' he repeated. 'But it weren't just about me and her. The school was after her, too, for taking time off unauthorised and all that. She'd been intercepting the phone calls. Ripping up the letters.'

'She wasn't the only one taking time off though, was she, Warren?'

He shrugged and looked away. It spoke volumes.

'So, how did you come up with fifty pounds a week then?'

'Saturday job. I even managed to get a few more shifts,' he said.

'It must have been pretty difficult,' she sympathised.

'Alicia helped out — whenever she could,' he muttered.

Casey persisted. 'But it must have been harder for you, having to part with all your money every week. I don't suppose your parents would reimburse you if you found yourself a bit short.'

Not if the story of the chocolate bars was anything to go by.

'All the money they make, though — Alicia's mum and dad. Fifty quid would be neither here nor there to them, would it?'

Warren stared down at the floor. Some internal debate was going on inside him. Casey waited.

'All right, all right,' he said at last. 'It was me what asked her to nick that gear from that posh shop. I just couldn't manage any more money. At first I wouldn't let her help out. It wasn't right, her being my girl.'

And who said chivalry was dead?

'If she'd have just hung on I'd have got away with it.' He slumped back in his chair.

'Got away with what exactly, Warren?'

He looked at her, startled. 'I wouldn't have had to give that Flynn woman any money, would I? Her being dead and all.'

'You've managed to save yourself an awful lot of money thanks to her murder, haven't you, Warren?'

Casey reached for her glass of water and drained it. Warren's gaze rested on the electric fan as it ineffectually churned the air and pulsed it back out no cooler. On and on it droned, until finally Warren drowned it out with his own voice.

'I think I want a solicitor,' he said, folding his arms.

* * *

The curtains at the front of the house were closed against the glare of the sun. Good, thought Drew — that meant she wouldn't have seen his car draw up.

Pushing open the front gate, Drew ambled up the drive and made his way round to the back door. On hot days like these, Catherine always left the door ajar. It was cheaper than air conditioning, she'd joke whenever he upbraided her for her cavalier attitude towards security.

When he discovered the door was locked, Drew was disappointed. Now he would have to knock and give the game away. The first attempt to get Catherine's attention came to nothing. Neither did the second. Drew took a few steps back and peered upwards in the direction of the back bedroom. Why were all the blinds and curtains drawn?

Although the temperature outside must have been hovering around the seventy-eight mark, Drew experienced the sudden grip of an icy hand upon his heart. Something wasn't right. Fumbling for the key she'd had made specially for him, he let himself inside, calling her name as he stumbled through the house, finally flinging open her bedroom door. In a second he took it all in — the empty pill containers scattered on the bedside table, the humming of a bluebottle so loud it drowned the rattle of his own lungs. And Catherine herself, still and grey in death, dressed in her nightgown, clutching an envelope in her hand.

* * *

Casey was getting nowhere fast. There was nothing — absolutely nothing — she could pin on Warren Smith that linked him with the murder of Sheila Flynn. In the end she'd had no alternative but to let him go. Now, as the evening cooled down at last, she stood at her bay window looking down on to the high street, a chilled glass of white wine in her hand. She was freshly showered and had changed out of her work clothes into a linen shirt and loose trousers.

She wished Dom were here. 'Well, ring him, you dope! Tell him you're sorry you couldn't return his call this morning but you were on your way to work.'

Technically that was the truth. She had been on her way to see Helen Shaw when Dom's name had flashed up on her phone this morning and she'd have been late if she had stopped to answer it. But what about all the other times she'd either ignored his calls or sent brief texts to say she was snowed under with work, and once her desk had cleared she would be back in touch? And then she never had.

All Dom had done was exactly what she'd more or less told him to do, which was to keep away. Couldn't he see she was only getting her retaliation in first? If there was any dumping to be done then she was going to be the one to do it.

But if she didn't return his call he'd be justified in being annoyed with her. If they were going to have a blow-up then it'd better be about something big. The possibility of Dom upping sticks to London was big.

'I'm a reasonable person,' she told herself as she pressed the button for Dom's name. It went straight to answerphone. Furious with herself for not having prepared some witty message in advance, she hurled the phone across the room.

What now? If she were to leave a message then they could be playing tag for the rest of the evening. She decided to phone his office number. Journalists, like the police, worked odd hours. There would be someone around who could tell her where Dom was.

The someone who picked up the phone was Dom's boss and editor of the *Brockhaven Gazette*, Al Sykes. Dom had a story and apparently it was a biggie, according to Al.

'Dead woman found. Local estate agent in love-rat triangle,' he said gleefully. 'Surprised you lot aren't on to it. Out Blakenthorpe way.'

'Look. Al, I'm good but I'm not that good,' she snapped back. 'I can't be everywhere at once. I happen to be investigating the murder of a local woman right now, so that the people of Brockhaven can once more sleep easy in their beds.'

He wasn't the only one who could do cliches.

'And exactly how well is your investigation coming along, Inspector Clunes?'

'Is this an interview?'

You had to be wary of journalists. Dom had told her that. They were never off duty — it was one more thing they had in common with the police.

'Because if it is perhaps you wouldn't mind returning the favour?'

In the end it had been tit-for-tat. Sykes had got his story — such as it was — and she'd got the details of Dom's whereabouts.

Flourishing her police ID, she managed to push her way through the small crowd that had gathered outside the house of the dead woman. So far there was no sign of Dom, though.

After a brief word with the PC on duty, she joined the Inspector who was sitting with a distraught man in his thirties, who was slumped at a table in the kitchen.

She recognised the man as Drew Shaw. She had seen his photograph when she'd been to interview Helen Shaw. Well, this was an interesting turn-up.

'I'm investigating the murder of Sheila Flynn,' she said to the Inspector. 'She used to work for this man and his family.'

Drew Shaw looked up at her, his eyes

wild and desperate. Casey struggled to suppress the image of his wife as she'd last seen her, fondly wiping the face of her son after he'd spread most of his breakfast over it. How many times had Drew Shaw done that in his life? she wondered, then suppressed the thought. It wasn't fair. She had no right to stand in judgment over another. That was the job of the courts.

There had been a suicide note. Running her eyes down the page, Casey quickly caught the drift of it. There was reference to a boy — Luke — and also to his untimely death.

It was through this bleak time I was prescribed these tablets but I refused to take them then. I couldn't understand why the medical profession were so keen to deny me my grief. Why did I hang on to them and not throw them away? Perhaps because I'd already chosen my path — had chosen it the moment I switched off Luke's life-support system.

There was much more — page after page through which she traced her relationship with Drew Shaw from its tentative beginnings to the moment they had reached now.

Never doubt that I loved you, Drew, the letter ended. *But I could never love you as much as you deserved. You were prepared to go to any lengths to keep us together. But I don't have your courage. Please forgive me. You must confess . . .*

'I think you should come with me back to Brockhaven, Sir,' Casey said. 'You might like to give me the name of your solicitor first.'

4

Casey needed to be on top form if she was going to get anywhere with Drew Shaw. Ten minutes peace and quiet was what she needed this morning. Ten more minutes in which to read and re-read Catherine Swinburne's suicide note.

> *You were prepared to go to any lengths to keep us together. But I don't have your courage. Please forgive me. You must confess.*

She'd read her final words over and over. To her, they meant one thing. But to a good solicitor? No doubt he'd be able to come up with any number of interpretations — all of which would get his client off the hook.

Last night she'd made some headway. After fifteen minutes of pussyfooting around, denying all knowledge of Sheila Flynn, bar the fact that she'd been employed by his wife, he'd finally come clean that she'd been blackmailing him.

'That doesn't make me a killer, Inspector,' he'd insisted.

'Maybe not,' she'd snapped back. 'But it gives me enough to keep you in a cell overnight while I check out your alibi.'

He hadn't argued with her. Maybe he felt safer in a cell than at home with his wife. Casey wouldn't blame him.

Up until the arrest of Shaw, Warren Smith had been her number-one suspect. He'd made no bones of the fact that he hadn't been able to stand Sheila Flynn and the anguish she'd been putting his girlfriend through. For him her death was a reason for rejoicing, not for grief. But was he a killer?

Her office phone rang shrilly just as someone began to knock on her door. Irritated at her train of thought being broken so abruptly, Casey snatched up the phone.

'DI Casey Clunes.'

'Why didn't you come and talk to me back at the suicide's house? You knew I was there covering the story for the paper.'

Blast! It was Dom.

'I'd just made an arrest. I wanted to get back to Brockhaven with him as soon as I could,' she said.

'Did he do it?'

'I don't know.'

'It was me who led you to that story, Casey. You owe me something!'

Casey hated being on the defensive. The only way out of this was to attack. 'This isn't a social call, then?'

Whoever was knocking on her door clearly had no intention of stopping till she answered it.

'I have to go. I've got an important interview,' she said, relieved to have a genuine excuse to get off the phone.

'So have I. That was partly why I was ringing you.'

Miraculously, the hammering on her door seemed to have stopped. It was contrary of her, but she willed it to start up again. She had a feeling that whatever Dom was about to tell her was going to make her wish she hadn't heard it.

'*The Independent* wants to see me. There may be a job.'

Casey stiffened. She should offer some words of congratulations at least. But nothing would come out.

'If I got it they would definitely expect me to move to London.'

It was impossible to read anything into his voice. She thought back to the day they'd taken that stroll down the pier. 'Don't you miss it, Casey? The buzz, being at the centre of everything?' So he'd finally been and gone and done it.

'If that's what you want, Dom,' she said, keeping her voice just as neutral as his own, 'then I hope you get it.'

She might have softened if he'd said, 'But what about you, what do you want?' But he didn't. Instead he muttered something about it being a great chance for him and he'd be a fool to ignore it. After that she shut her ears. Not that it stopped his words from riding roughshod over her heart. It was a relief when PC Walsh's head appeared round her door.

'I really do have to go,' she said, slamming down the receiver before he could finish telling her he'd let her know how he got on.

'This had better be important,' she snapped.

'It's Mr Flynn, ma'am. The husband of the deceased.'

'I know who he is, PC Walsh,' Casey said. 'Just get on with it.'

PC Walsh, taken aback by her sharpness, gulped the air like a fish. He normally got on very well with the Inspector.

'He wants to know when he can have his wife's body back. Keeps going on about a proper funeral and if you ask me I think he's losing it a bit.'

'Losing it! Of course he's losing it! His wife has just been murdered and her killer's still on the loose.'

Casey, on the point of losing it herself, ran her hands through her hair.

'Yes, ma'am.' PC Walsh fixed his eyes on the floor. 'I'll go and see him myself, shall I, ma'am? Tell him we're doing all we can, reassure him, that sort of thing.'

Casey rose from her chair and tugged down the hem of her linen jacket, an action that seemed to calm her. 'Excellent idea, PC Walsh,' she said.

'Now, if you'll let me get on?'

★ ★ ★

Ian Walsh wasn't looking forward to his encounter with George Flynn. There was nothing he could tell him that he hadn't already told him on the phone. Then he reminded himself he wasn't here to make himself feel any better.

It made him feel less like he was wasting his time, though, when he spotted Kevin Flynn's beat-up gas-guzzler parked outside. He hadn't been able to shake off the feeling that there was something a bit fishy about Flynn Junior when he'd been here with DI Clunes the first time.

'You'd better come in,' George Flynn said, opening the front door to admit PC Walsh.

Removing his hat, PC Walsh shuffled inside. The house was stuffy, the drawn curtains blocking out the sun.

'Sit down. I'll put the kettle on.'

Thank God for tea, PC Walsh thought,

clearing a space for himself on one end of the sofa.

'Isn't that your son's car outside?' he asked when, some three minutes later, Mr Flynn returned with two mugs of very weak tea. 'Aren't you making one for him?'

'Car's got something wrong with it. Don't ask me what,' Mr Flynn replied. 'It's something different every month.'

'Right.'

PC Walsh gazed down at the pale liquid. Had Mr Flynn even waited for the kettle to come to the boil? he wondered. Perhaps he should have volunteered to make it himself.

'How's your son coping, by the way?'

He was grateful for the opening. No point asking how the older man was coping. That was clear enough, from his grey, dishevelled appearance.

'Him and Sheila weren't that close,' Mr Flynn replied. 'Kevin blamed her for coming between Karen — his mum — and me.'

Ian's ears pricked up.

'No use telling kids though, is it? Me

218

and Karen were all washed up years before Sheila came on the scene. Sheila was the best thing that ever happened to me.'

'I'm very sorry, Mr Flynn. Please, if it's any consolation, we're doing everything we can . . . '

Mr Flynn blinked and waved the words away with a gesture.

'If you want I can arrange some bereavement counselling for you.'

'I don't need counselling, lad. I'll manage,' he said. 'I'm not on my own. I never thought I'd say it but Kevin's really come up trumps since Sheila died.'

Now Ian was suspicious. He made some banal comment about family being best at times like these, which Mr Flynn readily agreed with.

'I've had to insist he went out for a drink today — he hasn't left my side since you and that lady Inspector first came round on Friday,' he said.

Blimey! it was only Sunday morning now — hardly a huge act of self-sacrifice on Kevin's part, Ian thought.

'Hasn't been out since after you left,

when he slipped round the school to tell the office I wouldn't be in to do my shift. I was in a right state because there was things needed doing and Hollis — the other caretaker — he's off with his back.' Mr Flynn drained his tea and placed the mug on a pile of papers. 'Don't worry, Dad, give me the keys and I'll tidy up for you,' he said.'

Perhaps this hadn't been a wasted visit after all, PC Walsh mused as he drove back towards the station some fifteen minutes later — the soonest he'd felt able to make his escape.

Just why, on the day of his stepmother's death, had this young man, who, according to his own father was little more than a work-shy boozer, suddenly become so compassionate that he'd felt compelled to do his father's caretaking shift for him?

'Give me the keys,' he'd said. Keys to the school, no doubt. Keys to outhouses and boiler rooms and all sorts of secret places you could hide things, like murder weapons. It was time to get a search organised.

Twelve noon. Could it get any hotter? Yes, if the weather forecast were to be believed. Casey tapped her pencil against her teeth impatiently. Two suspects, both released. Where now?

She should have been relieved when Shaw's alibi — he'd been viewing a property out Brancaster way with a young couple at the time of Sheila's death — had played out. And now she'd thought more carefully about those words in the letter, she understood what Catherine Swinburne had really meant. It wasn't murder that Drew Shaw needed to confess to, but adultery. Well, he had no choice now but to do just that.

From having two suspects she now had none. Warren Smith had proved squeaky-clean, too. Students at Brockhaven High were marked present in a register at the start of every lesson. Warren hadn't missed a single class on Friday. Both his name and Alicia's had showed up as in class on time throughout the day.

So where now? It was a relief when the

duty sergeant, a plump-faced, roly-poly woman who took her role as mothering the troops seriously, burst in, scattering her thoughts.

'Young Walsh has radioed through,' she announced. 'Thinks he's got something on Kevin Flynn. I've organised a search of the school premises, Casey. You should get down there.'

★   ★   ★

Brockhaven High was an uninspiring building set in uninspiring grounds. Over the years, as the catchment area had grown, numerous extensions had been added, giving Casey the impression that it had been designed by an unimaginative child who'd been given a bucket of Lego for a present, which he'd stuck on at random till he'd used it all up.

At the same moment she drew up, a police van was disgorging a team of officers and two dogs. PC Walsh, his movements purposeful, his smooth, boyish face eager to get cracking, separated from the rest. As they disappeared round the back of the

222

school, he made his way over to where she stood.

'What do you know, Officer?'

She made her tone light. She felt bad about being so sharp with him earlier. Maybe, when all this was over, she'd buy him a drink and explain why. But as his expression melted into one of puppy-dog devotion, she decided against it. Oh, God, that was all she needed. How long would it be before half the nick cottoned on that Ian Walsh had fallen for her?

He made short work of explaining his suspicions. The caretaker's office was next to the boiler room. Kevin Flynn had definitely been there on the Friday evening, not long after the two of them had called on George Flynn with the news of his wife's murder.

'Lead me to the place. The sooner we start the quicker we'll be.'

The door to both the boiler room and the caretaker's office had already been unlocked as Casey and PC Walsh approached. The team of officers turned out cupboards and drawers with a methodical detachment. The dogs sniffed

round the boiler room equally deter-
minedly. If there was anything to be
found here then they'd find it.

'Come on, guys! I need some evidence!' Casey called out to the men.

As if in reply, one of the dogs barked
loudly and the officer who'd been raking
about in the remains of the boiler room
fire yelled out triumphantly. Casey rushed
over. She could just make out the charred
remains of what appeared to be a cricket
bat and a thick rope. Success!

'Get that lot over to Forensics,' she
ordered. 'And get Kevin Flynn down to
the nick.'

When her mobile rang she ignored it.
She was within sniffing distance of Sheila
Flynn's murderer — she didn't have time
for phone calls.

Back at the station, Casey hurried to
the interview room. PC Tony Lennon
scurrying behind.

It was a very subdued Kevin Flynn who
sat waiting for her.

'I don't know what this is about but
you ain't got nothing on me,' he said,
making a half-hearted attempt to stand as

Casey entered the room.

'Sit down, Mr Flynn. We'll do the preliminaries first, if you don't mind.'

Once the tape was set up, Casey began her questioning.

'What were you doing at Brockhaven High last Friday evening, Kevin?'

He tried to deny he'd been there but once Casey confronted him with his father's statement he decided to drop it.

'Like Dad said, I went down there to tell them he wouldn't be in. But there was no one there to tell. So I just tidied up a bit, like he told me to.'

'That was very noble of you, Kevin.'

'He's very particular is my dad,' he said.

Casey nodded graciously. Then she let him have it.

'Was your stepmother blackmailing you, Kevin?'

'You what?'

Either he had no idea what Casey was suggesting or he was a good actor. His expression was one of utter bewilderment.

There was a knock on the door. It was PC Walsh.

'The evidence has gone straight round to Forensics and they're working on it right now, ma'am,' he said officiously. 'Oh, and we thought you might like to have a look at this.'

The package PC Walsh handed her contained what must have been more than a thousand pounds' worth of cocaine. When he saw Casey's eyes widen he could barely contain his grin.

'And just where did you find this, Constable?'

'It was in a bucket, ma'am. Next to the disinfectant and a couple of mops.'

Flynn groaned from his seat.

'Looks like you lads have properly cleaned up, I'd say,' she said, regretting her unintended pun immediately it popped out. 'Put it on the table here and then you can go. Oh, and keep me informed of anything else you may come up with.'

'Yes, ma'am,' PC Walsh said, before leaving the room.

Casey turned to face Flynn. 'I wouldn't have had you down as a drugs baron,' she said, eyeing him beadily. He was sweating and shifty-eyed.

'Look,' Kevin said nervously. 'When they arrested me they said I was under suspicion of murdering Sheila. I'll put my hand up to this lot. I'll even give you the name of the bloke I got it from. But I don't know nothing about no blackmail and I know even less about murder.'

He was shaking now. Terrified.

'What were you doing at the school on Friday night, Kevin? We found evidence of what could be the weapon that killed your stepmother. Did you go to the boiler room to burn it?'

''Course I didn't! I went round the school to pick up that lot.' He eyed the bag of white powder nervously. 'I sell drugs, don't I? It's how I make my living.'

And how he fed his habit, too. A user, Casey was sure of it.

'Look. Let me go and I'll give you the name of the big guy. You don't want me. I'm nobody in this business.'

If they could catch whoever it was selling on drugs to small-time suppliers like Kevin, that wouldn't have been a bad thing. But it was a murderer Casey was after right now, not a drug dealer. Until they got something back from Forensics there was precious little they could hold Kevin for as far as Sheila Flynn's murder went.

Another sharp rap at the door and Walsh was in the room once more.

'I forgot something,' he said. 'Forensics, ma'am. They want to know why you didn't return their call. Something about a message on your mobile?'

Casey's mobile was back in her office. It was ringing as she entered. Lunging for it, all fingers and thumbs and her mind in a whirl, she grabbed it just in time. It was Forensics again. A number of tiny red sequins had been found at the scene and on the body. They were of a type you might find on fashion garments. Dresses, tops, that sort of thing.

A cold shiver ran the length of Casey's spine.

'And on shoes?' she said.

'Definitely. I'd have said so,' came the reply.

Thirty minutes later, she was inside the Endecotts' hallway. The smell of freshly ground coffee wafted through the house.

Mrs Endecott was alone with her daughter, she said. Sunday was Mr Endecott's golfing day.

'I'd like a word with Alicia, Mrs Endecott,' Casey said.

'What's this about, Inspector?' Mrs Endecott's tongue darted over her top lip nervously.

'Is she upstairs?'

Without waiting for an answer, she took the stairs two at a time. Alicia's room was easy to find. Ugly rap music pulsated from inside. Casey flung open the door.

'What the — !'

Alicia Endecott lay on her bed, still dressed in her pyjamas. Casey's eyes alighted on Alicia's sparkly turquoise ballet slippers.

'Nice slippers, Alicia,' she said. 'Now show me the red ones.'

Mrs Endecott came bustling into the room behind her, demanding to know what was going on.

'Did you buy your daughter a pair of red shoes similar to the ones she's wearing now, Mrs Endecott?' Casey demanded.

'Yes,' she said. 'She's got six pairs. Black, cream, those turquoise ones, and definitely red. She insisted on red. Can't remember the other colours, though.'

Casey supplied one of the colours herself. 'Orange,' she said, recalling what Alicia had been wearing when she'd been caught shoplifting. 'That's right,' Mrs Endecott said. 'Oh, and royal blue.

But why do you want to know, Inspector?'

Casey fixed her eye on Alicia, who was throwing shoes out of her wardrobe in a desultory manner.

'Can't seem to find my red ones anywhere,' she said insolently.

'Do you want me to tell your mum why I'm here, Alicia?' Casey said. 'Or are you going to tell her yourself?'

★   ★   ★

Alicia Endecott hadn't been a hard nut to crack in the end. On the contrary, it was as if she took delight in what she'd done. She'd had years at school of being bullied — and all because she could sound her aitches, she said bitterly.

'Warren had this reputation. I thought

he was hard. But it was all front. He wouldn't do anything to shut Sheila Flynn up, so I had to,' she admitted coolly, as she was led away.

Casey wondered about Warren. Had he known she'd done it, or had he been just as much in the dark about Sheila's murderer as everyone else? Whatever his tough image, in the end he'd been Alicia's patsy, putting up with her goading him to put an end to Sheila Flynn's little blackmailing game for weeks.

When he wouldn't do it, Alicia had simply decided to do it herself, arranging with another girl to call 'present' for her when the register was taken.

'None of the teachers look up when they check you off on the roll,' she'd said. 'It's dead easy to fool them. Well, most of them, anyway.'

★ ★ ★

An exhausted Casey, home at last, kicked off her shoes and slumped in a chair, images of Alicia Endecott in the act of murder crowding her head. Sheila Flynn was no angel. But had she really deserved to die so brutally? Alicia clearly thought so. Sheila Flynn was a bully and Alicia had had her fill of bullies. And when the boy she'd chosen to fight her battles for her let her down, she decided it was time to fight back.

Casey's downstairs bell rang shrilly. She leaned out of the window. It was Dom.

'Are you going to let me in?' he shouted, craning his neck upwards.

She could have said no — but she was tired of keeping up this ridiculous feud. The guy had applied for a job, and why shouldn't he? Had she ever given him even so much as a tiny hint that it mattered to her that he stuck around? It occurred to her that most men would have been long gone.

Locating her key, she threw it down to him. The sound of the key scratching at the door and his footsteps coming up the stairs seemed to last an age.

'Hi,' he said at last.

He held out a bottle of champagne. Casey's heart sank.

'What are we celebrating?' she asked him, her voice small. 'Your new job?'

'I haven't been for the interview yet. I might not even get it,' he said.

'You will.'

'You sound like you don't want me to,' he said.

'You wouldn't stand in my way, would you? If I fancied a change, I mean? So why should I stand in yours?'

Dom smiled. 'So if it's not the job, what is it?'

Imperceptibly, they both took a step towards each other.

'I don't want you to move to London if it means I'll never see you again,' she said, her words coming out in a rush.

'That's as near a declaration of love as I've ever had,' Dom said.

'I suppose it is,' she said. 'Are you going to open it then?' she added.

Because it looked like they had something to celebrate after all.